Bluegrass Bountiful

Dorothy,

Thanks for all your support & love through the years. Hope you enjoy the story.

Love
Fonda

Bluegrass Bountiful

by

Lozi Hart

[signature: Lozi Hart]

Turquoise Morning Press
Turquoise Morning, LLC
www.turquoisemorningpress.com

Turquoise Morning, LLC
P.O. Box 43958
Louisville, KY 40253-0958

Bluegrass Bountiful
Copyright © 2011, Lozi Hart
Print ISBN: 9781937389048

Cover Art Design by Kim Jacobs

Digital release, May 2011
Print release, June, 2011

Bluegrass Bountiful

Graham McCullough never forgot his first Kentucky Derby or the dark-haired beauty who stole his heart that weekend twenty-five years ago. He'd gone home to Scotland after the Derby intending to return to Louisville to ask the woman to be his wife. But a family crises sent him to the wilds of the Amazon Rain Forest for the next six months and when he finally did make it back, she had vanished without a trace.

Mary Claire Beaumont lived each day with a reminder of the weekend she'd spent with Graham McCullough, oh so long ago, before he'd disappeared from the face of the earth. She'd gone home to her mother and father prepared to face life as a single parent with an illegitimate child—until her mother forced her marriage to old boyfriend, John Beaumont. Now twenty-five years later, her daughter grown, a widowed Mary Claire is ready to live her own life, until fate throws Graham McCullough straight into her path again.

Prologue

Louisville, Kentucky
The First Saturday in May 1979

Mary Claire Rutherford stomped her bare foot on the folded beach towel covering the hot surface, then held her breath as her wobbly perch threatened to collapse. "I still can't see it!"

The last strains of *My Old Kentucky Home* faded from the speakers. Mary Claire looked around for anything else she could use to add height to the viewing stand she'd constructed, an old metal cooler stacked on top of multiple six-packs. She needed to hurry. The post parade was nearly over.

"Don't tell me you're actually here to see the race?"

Mary Claire turned to see who had spoken. Ah, the tall one with the muscles and no shirt. The one with the Scottish name that she knew she'd heard before. He'd caught her attention earlier when he'd shucked his clothes to reveal those ugly baggy swimming trunks just before diving headlong onto the Slip-n-Slide a group of frat boys had set up.

"Yeah." She jumped off the cooler. "I watch it every year, but this is my first time in the infield. I didn't realize I wouldn't be able to see from here."

"Tell you what." He stooped down and held up his hand. "Climb on my shoulders. That should give you a proper view."

"Oh yeah, right."

"Really, come on. They're almost to the gate."

She glanced toward the track and then down at him. She did want to see this race. "Oh, what the hell." She hitched her short-shorts up to the crease at the top of her legs, grasped his hand, and climbed on.

He raised straight up as if she weighed nothing at all. "How's that? Can you see now?"

"Yes." She wiggled, settling herself into the curve of his neck and shoulders.

Mary Claire put a hand above her eyes to shade them from the sun. The starter's bell sounded and the gate burst open spewing a frenzy of horse flesh onto the track.

Bluegrass Bountiful broke from the number nine position and stayed just behind the leaders until they reached the quarter pole. Mary Claire held her breath, her heart pounding as she watched the horse make his move.

"Come on Bountiful. You can do it." She yelled as the Rutherford Red Silks zoomed into the lead. "Yes, yes, yes!" Mary Claire bounced up and down on her shoulder seat. She waved her arms in the air still cheering as the chestnut stallion crossed the finish line three lengths ahead of his nearest competitor.

Mary Claire laughed, elated with the success. Bountiful had gone off at fourteen to one. That meant as soon as she cashed in her ticket, she'd be twenty-eight hundred dollars richer, enough to give her at least another eight months of living expenses. Besides, even if she wasn't speaking to her parents, she still wanted their Derby entry to win.

She had a special connection to this horse. She'd been in the barn the night Bountiful Bonny had foaled the much anticipated colt by Bluegrass King. Mary Claire had helped exercise and groom him and even slept in his stall on occasion. Her only regret was that she wouldn't be in the winner's circle today to congratulate Bluegrass Bountiful and slip him a sugar cube.

Graham McCullough stooped down again; this time to let the jubilant woman off his shoulders. She was flushed and smiling when she faced him.

He reached out and touched her arm. "It's been a real pleasure to have you riding me screaming *yes*. How about we position you a bit lower and try it again?" He knew he shouldn't have said it as soon as it came out of his mouth, but too much alcohol and too little food had stifled his better judgment.

He felt the sting of her hand across his face before he ever saw it coming. "Ouch!" He massaged his cheek as he watched her grab up a pair of leather sandals, stuff them into a floral print tote bag, and stalk off toward the entrance to the tunnel that went under the track, out of the infield, and toward the grandstand that stood beneath the twin spires of Churchill Downs.

Thunder rumbled in the distance. The storm was moving closer and Graham was still wandering around the streets of Louisville in a neighborhood that, like him, had seen better days.

He'd been wearing only his bathing trunks when he woke up an hour or so ago. The incredibly small tee shirt he'd managed to stretch over his upper half and the flip-flops that slapped against his heels as he walked he'd found in the discarded debris of the hordes who invaded Louisville on Derby day. He didn't have a clue what had happened to his own clothes or his wallet and cash.

After Miss Legs had tagged his jaw and stomped off, he'd stopped drinking beer and gone for the mint juleps—the signature drink of the day—only without the mint or the julep part. He'd been gulping straight bourbon during the final two races.

He vaguely remembered his friend, Robbie, saying the rest of them were going on to the hotel and Graham could catch up with them later. Only thing was, Graham wasn't driving. He was only along for the ride this trip, so he hadn't bothered to ask the name of the hotel.

He'd watched Miss Legs all afternoon in that scoop neck, sleeveless tee and those damned short-shorts up to her…. Graham shook his head to get the image out of his mind.

Her skin had been silky smooth, and oh, the way she'd smelled. The perfume she wore was the real thing—subtle and expensive.

It began to sprinkle. He looked up trying to determine if a downpour was imminent as he passed by the window of a small storefront diner. A glimpse of something inside caught his eye. He stopped. A floral print tote bag sat in a chair at the table by the window.

He recognized it because he'd given one like it as a birthday gift to his sister, Polly. He'd bought it in Paris at the Laura Ashley Shop. He smiled as he silently repeated, *Paris, France not Paris, Kentucky*, the way he and Polly had always done for their Kentucky born mother. It had become a McCullough family joke. He reached for the door handle and hesitated only a moment before he pulled it open and entered the building.

The walls of the little diner were lined with continuous rows of framed black and white photographic prints. Including ones taken at the very counter where a shabbily dressed old man and Miss Legs now sat.

She was deep in conversation with a man behind the counter who swiped at the surface of the bar with a wet rag. He wore an apron that may have been white a few years ago.

All three turned to look at Graham.

The man in the apron stopped in mid-swipe, raised the hand that held the rag, and pointed toward the door. "Keep on going, my friend. We're all out of leftovers. I'm ready to lock up."

Miss Legs did a double take and laughed. "You look a little worse for wear this evening."

"Can I talk to you for a minute?" He pointed to the table by the window. "Over here."

She hesitated then slid off the stool. "Sure, why not?" She walked to the table where the tote bag sat.

He pulled the chair out and waited for her to sit down.

"Oh, so we're a gentleman now?" She remained standing.

He dipped his head and felt his cheeks warm with embarrassment. "I…I'm really sorry about that comment. It's no excuse I know, but I plead intoxication. I do apologize."

She pursed her lips and then nodded. "Accepted." She sat down.

He stayed behind her and helped scoot the chair in before he sat down across from her.

He cleared his throat. "I…I hate to ask, but I need a favor."

She raised her eyebrows. "And what would that be?"

"Can I borrow some money? I seem to have lost my funds along with my clothes. I only need enough for a hotel room tonight and to buy something to wear tomorrow."

She gave a snort of laughter. "Did you hit your head today? You surely must realize there's not an empty hotel room within a hundred miles of here. Besides, I don't have any to lend you." She started to get up, scrutinized his face, hesitated, then settled back into the chair.

Graham dropped his head. *He was screwed.* He knew he'd never get in touch with his dad. He was three weeks into a trip in the wilds of the Amazon Rain Forest. Graham looked at the clock. And, it was already well into Sunday in Great Britain. He'd play hell trying to find someone to wire him money.

"Well, then, do you know of anyplace close I could hang out for the next couple of days, out of the rain?" His stomach rumbled. "And maybe get a bit to eat?"

She rose all the way up this time and walked to the counter. "Burl, where's that camera you keep handy?"

"In the drawer, where it always is." The man in the apron answered.

"May I borrow it for a minute?"

Burl wiped his hands on the bib of his apron, took the 35 mm from its resting place and handed it to her.

She crossed the room again. She circled Graham, snapping pictures as she went then took the camera back to Burl. "Thank you." She handed him the camera.

Miss Legs smiled as she turned and walked back to the table. Her eyes locked with Graham's as she said in a loud clear voice. "Burl, if anything happens to me in the next couple of days, make sure you take those pictures to the police."

She picked up her bag. "Come on. You can sleep on my sofa tonight. I may even let you have a peanut butter sandwich if you behave yourself."

****

Mary Claire didn't look back but she was sure he was following as she made a mad dash across the street toward the empty building that had once housed a four-story department store. She used a key to open a door tucked away to the right of a row of boarded up display windows. She locked the door behind them. A dim light filtered down from above. He still followed as she made her way up a flight of stairs to an open landing and then stepped into an old freight elevator. The cage swung and clanged against the sides of the shaft before it settled again.

He hesitated. "This thing looks ancient. Are you sure it'll support both of us?"

She smiled at him and shrugged. "Suit yourself." She slid the gate closed. "Stairs are over there." She pointed to a door at the far side of the landing. "You'll need to go all the way to the top. And be careful. It's pretty dark in there." She pulled the control lever and began her ascent.

Mary Claire laughed out loud. She finally remembered who he was. Graham McCullough, heir to the Castleton-McCullough British industrial and textile empire. Rich boy on an adventure in the colonies before he settled into the corporate world to become *Daddy-in-Training. Daddy* in this instance, being William McCullough, a name forbidden to be uttered in the Rutherford household.

The mere mention of the name McCullough was enough to send her father into an apoplectic fit! Something about an old family feud carried here from Scotland almost a hundred years ago. Ancient history in Mary Claire's book. What possible importance could it still hold?

Her oldest brother, Ben, would do the same some-day, take over the family business, now that Daddy was over being mad at him for marrying an atheist. Hank, the brother just older than Mary Claire, would keep the equine interests going. But she'd be damned if she was going to do what everyone expected and marry John Beaumont.

John was nice, but he was boring. And Mary Claire knew she'd never be able to pursue her art career if she married him. He'd want her to be like his mother and her mother, hosting dinners and parties and afternoon get-togethers to showcase their husbands business interests.

And even if she was living rent-free in a building her father owned, by God, she was going to make her own way. Her sculptures that were already in private collec-tions were getting good remarks in the local art commu-nity. A few more months and she'd have enough pieces to do an exhibit. That should at least let her earn enough to really be on her own.

The elevator stopped. She opened the gate, flipped on the lights and made a quick survey of the apartment. A trail of water droplets marked her path. She snatched up everything that referred to her name—no sense opening that can of worms if the McCulloughs hated the Rutherfords as much the Rutherfords hated the McCulloughs—and stuffed it all into a leather-covered storage box.

She went into the bathroom, grabbed a towel and patted the rain water off her arms and legs, then pulled the clasp from her hair and wrapped the towel around her head. It was another two minutes before he pounded on the door. She unlocked the door and swung it open.

"That wasn't nice." He strode through the opening.

She shrugged. "I was dripping. I didn't feel like standing around all night while you conquered your fear."

"That stairwell was black as pitch."

"I told you to be careful." She went to the cabinet and took out a jar of peanut butter and a loaf of bread and laid them on the counter. "Knives are in the drawer by the sink. Enjoy."

She went to the bedroom and retrieved a couple of sheets and a pillow. She threw them on the sofa. "Bathroom's through there." She pointed to the enclosed space. "Goodnight."

****

God! What was that annoying noise? Graham jerked at the sheet and opened his eyes to the darkness. Clink. Clink. Thud. Clink. Clink. He sat up and looked around. The dial of a lighted clock radio on the desk read 3:10. Ugh. He lay back down and there it was again. Thud. Thud. Clink. Clink. Clink. He stood up and pulled on his trunks, looking around.

Lightning streaked across the night sky. *Boom.*

After the roll of thunder subsided he listened closer. The sound was coming from behind the wall by the desk. He went toward the wall and found a door.

The space on the other side was as big as a gymnasium. Windows covered two walls. The wall with the door hosted a make-shift office space. The other wall looked like it had been transported from a library; rows of shelves were filled with books and objets d' arte. The floor was covered by a montage of sculpture in a variety of mediums and Miss Legs was smack in the middle of it, banging away with a hammer and chisel.

She had on fuzzy, pink, feather-trimmed slippers, a lacy, white, calf-length night gown, and, safety goggles.

Her dark curly hair frizzed above and below the goggles. She looked, for all the world, like a deranged mutant insect and she was so focused on her work she didn't even notice him.

"Don't you sleep?"

She screamed and jerked, causing the chisel to miss the stone and go flying across the room when the force of the hammer hit it. She dropped the hammer and ripped off the goggles.

"Damn it! You almost caused me to ruin it. What are you doing up?"

"It's a little hard to sleep with all that banging going on."

"I'm…sorry." She stooped down to retrieve the goggles that had fallen to the floor. She laid them on her work bench then ignored him as she picked up a broom and dust pan and began to sweep up bits and pieces of stone.

He moved around the room examining the sculptures, careful not to step on any stray bits of stone as he went. The workmanship impressed him.

"Did you do all of this?"

"Yes." She didn't raise her head from her housekeeping task.

"A bit eclectic in style. And so many different mediums."

"Oh, and now you're an art expert?" She raised up and shot him a withering stare.

"Just an observation. No criticism intended." He moved closer to her.

"What's your name?" He ran a hand across the granite breast of a life-size female figure.

She didn't answer only exhaled in a huff and resumed her sweeping.

He picked up a book from a stand close to the work bench. Poe. He looked again at the pieces he had just walked by, a marble bust of a mustachioed man with lank, collar-length hair, a black bird in metal and a limestone disc with a bleeding heart centered in relief.

"Who's that?" He pointed to the piece she had been working on.

She laid the broom on the floor then walked to her work bench still carrying the dustpan. She unlocked the turntable and whirled it around so he could see the face. "This is Annabel Lee."

"So you're doing all the characters from Poe's writing?"

"No, just my favorites. I've already done a number of Shakespeare," she glanced toward the marble woman he had fondled a moment ago. She emptied the dustpan, then set it beside the broom. "After I finish Poe, I'm going to start on Beowulf and Grendel."

"It's an interesting concept. How did you come up with it?"

She talked about her art until a brilliant flash of lightning caused her to stop short. She slid off the stool and went to the window. Graham came over to stand behind her.

"This round of storms is moving in fast." She rested her palms on the stone window sill.

"Is the weather here always so volatile?"

She shook her head. "Only in spring." She paused. "And summer and winter."

He laughed. "And autumn." He said it with her.

She glanced around at him and smiled then turned her attention back to the nature show. A blinding flash of light and a building ratting kaboom caused her to shriek and whirl around, away from the window, landing her face straight into his bare chest.

Darkness surrounded them. He wrapped his arms around her. "Wow, that was spectacular." He tightened his hold. She didn't try to move away. The wind buffeted against the windows. When the lightning flashed he could see the few trees along the sidewalk bending low under its force.

He felt the rapid beat of her heart against his chest. It wasn't slowing. "Are you afraid the storm?" His voice was quiet in the darkness.

Her face brushed against his chest, moving from side to side. "No."

His voice was even softer as he asked the next question. "Are you afraid of me?"

She raised her face to him. "No." She said again.

He leaned down and kissed her. Her lips were soft and warm. Her arms slid around his neck and she pressed herself against him. He broke the kiss and held her away from him, searching her face in the intermittent light.

"I can't plead intoxication this time, but my beautiful Annabel Lee, the offer still stands. What do you say?"

She took his hand and led him around the perimeter of the darkened space.

"My bed is this way."

Chapter One

Graham McCullough was meeting his youngest son for breakfast. Whatever in the world had convinced Sean that he needed to get his education at the University of Kentucky, Graham would never figure out. But then why should he know? He hadn't been much involved in his sons' lives for the past twelve years. Since he and Barbara had finally called it quits.

Graham walked out of the hotel and looked up. The air was cool this morning but the clear, blue bowl of a sky promised the afternoon would heat up.

He started off toward the café. The early morning quiet of the downtown streets soothed him. Lexington was straining so hard to become a big city. Graham hoped they didn't accomplish it. He liked the small town atmosphere it still evoked. He'd even bought a house close by.

He now owned a building with a three thousand square foot penthouse apartment and a farm with a twenty thousand square foot house and he was living out of a hotel. The furniture for the apartment was scheduled for delivery tomorrow. That would help. He hated hotel living.

Kentucky was special to Graham. His mother was raised in Danville and they'd visited often while his grandparents were still alive, though it'd been twenty years or so since his last trip.

Graham took a deep breath. He was excited by the prospect of this new venture he and Hamish MacDougal, his overseer of corporate operations, were embarking upon. Graham had spent the last three months conducting business by international phone calls, setting up an office here, and buying the farm.

This particular farm, with its monstrosity of a house now fallen into disrepair, had been a late entry in his U.S. business plan. He'd toyed with the idea of trying to buy it for a few years. Then when Sean had announced he'd be coming to Lexington, Graham had launched an all out offensive to find the present owner and buy the place. Maybe Sean would want to live there someday in the American ancestral home of the McCulloughs. The American ancestral home of the McCulloughs *and* the Rutherfords.

Graham wondered how long he could avoid a run-in with the Rutherford family's current patriarch. Probably not long, considering he was in their stomping grounds and about to infringe on their sacred industry. Graham remembered his father describing the man thirty years ago as a hard-nosed old bastard "who'd drown little biddies in the creek"—another of the curious expressions Graham's mother had introduced into their vocabulary.

Actually, it had been twenty-three years since he'd been in the Commonwealth. He remembered his last futile, desperate trip. His final foray through Louisville looking for her, for Annabel Lee, three weeks before he and Barbara had married.

He stopped and waited for a traffic light to change before he crossed the street. The café where he and Sean were to meet was just ahead.

He should warn Sean of the dangers this part of the world held for a young man. He should tell his son to beware of dark haired Cassandra's who stole your heart and left a hole in your soul so big a Mac truck could drive through it.

But he wouldn't. Because to do that would admit to the boy that Graham had never loved his mother. He'd been fond of Barbara and a few times was even convinced that he did love her. But inevitably, he'd find himself comparing her to the one who'd got away, to his Annabel Lee. He entered the café and chose a seat close to the window.

That had been one hell of a year. Graham had not only spent the night after the Kentucky Derby with his erstwhile sculptor, but the next two days as well. He'd left on Tuesday morning with every intent of flying back the next week to convince her to tell him her real name and to marry him. Then on Saturday the call had come from South America.

His father's expedition hadn't been heard from for two weeks and had missed their last three check-points. Graham had spent six months flying in and out of every country along the route they were supposed to have taken, before Hamish had convinced him to end the search.

When Graham had finally made it back to Louisville, she was gone without a trace. The little diner across the street from her building was closed and boarded up and no one else in the neighborhood seemed to know anything about her.

Graham had spent the ensuing twenty plus years as CEO of Castleton-McCullough Industries, traveling the world and scouring every art gallery he passed along the way, looking for anything he thought was a literary character, something that would prove she had been real.

He *wasn't* an art expert, but he had been surrounded by fine things from birth, and he could tell even then—though her career was only in it's infancy—she possessed a rare talent, one that should have catapulted her into the ranks of the elite in the art world. But in all his years of searching, he had found not one trace, not one shred of evidence that she still existed.

It had been a bitter pill to swallow, losing his father and her in the same year. He'd gone home and buried himself in the business. Graham had kept Hamish as operations overseer, the same position he'd filled for Graham's father. With Hamish's experience and Graham's fresh perspective on business, the company had thrived, grown, and then skyrocketed. Now they were expanding again, diversifying. That's what had brought him back to Kentucky after all these years.

Graham stared out the window. He saw Sean coming down the sidewalk. Sean was a good looking boy. He favored Barbara's family, her brother, Robbie, in particular.

Sean smiled when he saw his father. Graham stood as his son came to the table. He held out his hand and the young man shook it.

The waitress brought coffee and took their order.

"You're looking well." Graham took a sip of his coffee. "How's your mother?"

"Fine. I talked to her last night and told her you were visiting today. She sends her best."

Graham took another sip of coffee then nodded his head.

"Dad," Sean leaned across the table, "it's okay, you know."

"What?"

"It's okay that you and Mom are divorced. I like both of you a lot better now than I did when I was a kid." He sat back. "The two of you were miserable together. And you made Jamie and me miserable too." Sean picked up his coffee cup. "Why'd you get married anyway? I know it wasn't a have-to case."

Graham smiled as he stared into his cup then looked up at Sean. "It was time. Both our families were constantly harping about it. We'd dated off and on for years. And we didn't hate each other, so we got married."

"Well that's a really good reason." Sean laughed.

"We thought it was." Graham looked at his son, a grown man, much wiser than he'd been at the same age.

"So you and Hamish are going into the horse business, huh?"

Graham nodded. "Hamish swears he knows as much about horses as he does about the textile industry. Besides, we thought since we produce so much fabric for the racing silks, we might as well design our own."

"Well, the Keeneland sale is the place to start." Sean drained the contents of his cup. "I hope you find the horse you're looking for."

****

Mary Claire Beaumont was hard at work. She scooped up another fork full of soiled straw and tossed it on the pile outside the stall. She'd been mad as hell when Hank had called at four o'clock this morning, begging her to help.

That idiot he'd hired to drive the van had wrecked on the way to the track. Eight barn workers were injured, four in the hospital and the other four too banged up to work. Hank had been scrambling big time trying to find warm bodies to fill the slots. Things had to be pristine today. Mary Claire surveyed her work and gave a satisfied nod. She was keeping these stalls so clean, the money men could pretend that horses didn't poop if they wanted.

She was actually enjoying the workout and being around the horses. A lot of years had passed since she'd mucked stalls. Though she had started sculpting again, it had been ages since she'd done anything close to manual labor. John had always thought it degrading. He was probably rolling over in his grave right about now.

Mary Claire heard the sound of a buying party approaching, as she tossed another fork full onto the pile. She turned and took two steps further into the stall, then froze in mid-stride. She must be hearing things. She shook her head, stopped and listened again. Dear God, it couldn't be. Not after all these years. She stood stock still and then held her breath, trying to listen more intently. It couldn't be, but it was. It had to be, there was no mistaking that voice. She tried to hide, disappear into the stall.

Graham stopped dead in his tracks. He looked her up and down, taking in her disheveled appearance, at her curly hair trying to escape its pony tail confinement. He opened his mouth to speak but no sound came out. Finally he just smiled.

"Graham, are you coming?" His companions stopped a few feet beyond where Graham was standing.

"Go ahead. I'll be right there." He waited until the other two men were out of earshot before he spoke to her.

"So what happened?" He stared at the pile of hay and manure. "Did the bottom fall out of the sculpture business?"

Her heart was pounding so hard she could barely hear his words above the sound of the blood thumping her ears. She willed herself to calm down but could still hear the thud when she finally did manage to speak.

"Actually... I'm...I'm getting ready to start...start a series of pieces on thoroughbreds. So I thought what better way to get close to them? The track gets a few days free labor, and I get my research material." *Okay, that sounded plausible, even if she was lying through her teeth.*

"You look good, Annabel."

"Liar. I look like crap. Probably smell like it too."

"Can you get away later? For lunch?"

"No." She shook her head. "I don't have a change of clothes with me. And I'm sure most people aren't that fond of essence of horse barn wafting through the air while they're dining."

Mary Claire followed his glance in the direction his companions had gone. They were already through the center passage way of the next barn, motioning for him to come on.

He turned back to look at her. "Will you be here this evening?"

"Depends on how long it takes for all the buyers expected at this barn to show up."

He laid his hand against her arm. "Stay. I need to talk to you."

Even through the cotton fabric of her shirt, his touch felt like a fire-brand. Her insides were churning when she raised her eyes to meet his. "Why? Louisville was a long time ago."

"Please just stay. I'll be back." He turned away from her and hurried to catch up with the other two men.

Mary Claire sat on a bench outside the barn. This was not a good idea. She must be insane sitting here waiting for a man that, until this morning, she hadn't laid eyes on in twenty-five years. She couldn't believe he still held such an attraction for her. That voice and those eyes. Oh, those eyes.

She'd done some pretty fancy verbal tap-dancing a little while ago when Hank had offered to buy her dinner…trying to explain why she couldn't go without telling him the real reason.

Now it was getting dark. She was tired, she smelled bad, and she was beginning to think Mr. McCullough was as big a liar as she.

She got up and headed toward the parking lot, when she heard the crunch of tires on the gravel behind her. She turned as a black Lincoln Town Car stopped beside her. Graham opened the door and got out.

"I was afraid you'd give up on me."

"I did. I was on the way to my car."

"Sorry. My business took longer than I thought." He shifted his weight from one foot to the other.

Her mouth crooked into a smile. *He was nervous!*

"So, you ready to go?" He stood aside giving her room to slide into the front seat of the car.

Her smile turned into an expression of incredulity. "Ready to go? Look at me. I'm filthy. I can't go any-where."

"Oh, don't worry. I took care of that."

"How?"

"Come with me and I'll show you." He put his hand out toward the open car door, indicating that she should get in.

She studied his face and saw an expression of long-ing there like the one she hoped she was hiding on her own face. She shrugged and then instead of sliding in from the driver's side, walked around to the passenger side and got in.

They drove for half an hour in silence before he spoke. "Are you married?"

She turned her head and studied his profile. "Well, you must think mighty highly of yourself. Do you really think I'd be in this car with you right now if I were?"

"No."

Another minute passed.

"I was married. He died three years ago." She was staring straight ahead.

Graham glanced over at her. "I'm sorry."

"Thank you."

"Any kids?"

She considered stopping the conversation right now, insist that he take her back to her car, but they'd driven too far for that to be practical.

"One." She finally answered. "A daughter."

"I've got two boys. Sean, the youngest is in his first year here at university."

"Which university?"

"What do you mean which university? The University of Kentucky, of course."

"Well, there are several others close by. What is he studying?"

"Engineering."

"You said he was the youngest. What about the other one?"

"Jamie. James, as his mother calls him. He's back home. He studied business in London. He's getting his feet wet in the corporate world as my deputy director of finance."

Her hands clenched into fists. "So you're still married?"

"No. Divorced twelve years ago."

She relaxed.

He turned off the highway onto a two-lane road. They drove for another two miles and then turned onto an even more narrow paved lane before turning onto a gravel road. A short distance up the graveled road the remnants of a stone gateway, now fallen into disrepair, came into view. A little further and the outlines of a huge house became visible.

Soft light spilled from the windows of the ground floor. Graham pulled up close to the house and stopped the car.

Mary Claire didn't wait for him to open her door. She got out slowly. Her muscles were already stiffening from the unaccustomed workout they'd had today.

He opened the front door and took her hand. He led her through the foyer and down a long hallway into an elliptical space that had probably at one time been a ballroom.

Lit candles outlined the perimeter of the room. Inside the circle of light there was an old copper bathtub with steam rising from the water. Several department store boxes were piled beside a straight-backed side chair and off to the left was a stack of what looked to be three king-size mattresses, covered with white sheets and strewn with pillows.

"Your bath and fresh clothing." He pointed to the boxes by the chair. "Please enjoy it, while I see to our dinner."

She snorted. "You expect me to just strip down and climb into that tub in the middle of this huge room with no curtains on the windows and God knows who lurking in the shadows?"

"Yes."

"I don't think so." She crossed her arms over her chest. "I mean it's beautiful and romantic and a nice gesture and all that, but I'm really not an exhibitionist. And I'm not even going to ask about that!" She pointed to the bed. "I think you can take me back to Keeneland now."

"But... I thought we could..."

He was talking to her back as she stalked from the room headed for the car.

Chapter Two

Mary Claire pulled her white Lexus into a downtown parking space then looked across the street. She checked the address on the card to make sure the building was the right one.

Of course he couldn't just lease an office space in one of the multitude of new buildings springing up all around the outskirts of the city. No, he had to find a landmark in the heart of town and completely refurbish the structure. She noted that he'd been sure to omit any mention of the McCullough name on the building's signage when she finally located the understated, carved stone set into the brickwork on the left side. It simply read, Albion LTD. A wise move here in the middle of Rutherford country.

She'd spent the six days since she'd seen Graham trying to decide what she should do. They'd ridden back to the track that evening in relative silence. He talked. She didn't. She hadn't said a single word.

He'd tried to apologize six, maybe seven times and then draw her into a conversation, but she didn't budge. She'd maintained her stony silence. He'd thrust the card into her hand as she got out of the car. "Please call me," he'd pleaded.

Down deep she felt horribly guilty for giving him the silent treatment, for acting like he'd offended her. The truth was she'd wanted nothing more than to strip stark naked and drape herself spread-eagle across the bed for him. And then, while they were driving back, she'd had visions of both of them frolicking naked in the bathtub. She'd actually had to fan herself. She wasn't sure if she'd been having her first hot-flash or if it was just the residue of her imagining.

But as much as she may have wanted to, she couldn't let herself be swept away by Mr. Graham McCullough. Not again, not now. She was no longer twenty-year-old Mary Claire Rutherford, playing at being a bohemian sculptor. She was Mary Claire Beaumont, widow of renowned banker, John Beaumont; mother of a grown daughter; daughter-in-law of Sissy Beaumont, the social matriarch of central Kentucky. But most tellingly, she was the daughter of Clay Rutherford to whom the very name, McCullough was anathema. Clay Rutherford, who would interpret any association with a McCullough as the most heinous of betrayals.

She got out of the car and smoothed the front of her skirt. She picked up her handbag from the front seat and shoved the door closed, then crossed the street.

After he'd given her the card, she'd done some investigating. When she found out he'd bought the building and had set up his private office there, she knew she needed to do something—take control, get the upper hand, set the ground rules. Something! In a city the size of Lexington, it was inevitable that they'd run into each other sooner or later.

She entered the building and read the directory hanging on the wall. She took the elevator to the fifth floor, to the corporate office of Albion LTD.

****

Graham was wading through the sea of paper on his desk. Two boxes had arrived this morning containing the files and documents he needed to conduct his business here. He'd barely made a dent in the pile, and it was already past one o'clock in the afternoon.

His phone buzzed.

"Yes, Brooke, what is it?"

"Mr. McCullough, there's a Mrs. Mary Claire Beaumont here to see you."

He took off his reading glasses, put his hand up to his tired eyes, and squeezed them closed for a second. He opened them, then looked at the stack of paper again.

The last thing he needed was to spend an hour exchanging pleasantries with some genteel Southern lady about the importance of the arts in education or the plight of retired race horses or making sure the homeless had access to country ham and beaten biscuits or whatever cause this one was championing. He'd been besieged this past week. And it always came down to the final question. How much would he like to contribute?

"Have her make an appointment for later in the week, Brooke. I'm swamped this afternoon." He clicked the button on the phone.

He reached for another document when the phone buzzed again.

"Mr. McCullough, she says it's important. She says it's about a statue, a bust of Annabel Lee?"

Graham didn't bother to answer. He jumped up and practically ran to the door. He opened it and what he saw shocked him more than he would have believed possible.

Standing there was a perfectly coiffed lady, dressed in Donna Karan, carrying a Coach leather handbag. The couldn't be his Annabel Lee. No, his Annabel Lee had frizzy, fly-away hair. She wore short-shorts, pink fuzzy slippers, and safety goggles or blue jeans and work boots. His Annabel Lee could pound stone into submission and shovel horse shit! This woman, this Mary Claire Beaumont, looked like she'd never been dirty in her entire life.

"Hello," she said.

"Hi." He was staring. "I'm sorry. Please, please come in." He motioned to his office. "Brooke, hold my calls."

"Yes, sir."

He started to take Mary Claire's arm and then pulled his hand back. He closed the door instead. "Have a seat." He gestured to the pair of matching, black leather wingchairs angled towards his desk.

She arranged herself on the edge of one of the chairs. He sat in the matching one.

"Mary Claire Beaumont?"

She nodded.

"Proper southern name."

"Graham, I'm sorry."

"For what?"

"For acting so childish. About my name and…and the other night. For giving you the silent treatment."

"I guess I deserved it. It was presumptuous. I realize that now." He looked at her sitting there all prim and proper, on the edge of the chair with her hands folded in her lap, her legs from the knees down, at a slant to where they crossed at the ankles. He couldn't believe she'd ever been in insatiable goddess he'd spent an unforgettable three days with a lifetime ago.

"Graham, I would like to see you again. Socially, I mean. But there are considerations, concessions that will have to be made, dictated by my circumstances."

He gave her an appraising look. He wondered just how deep his Annabel Lee was buried beneath this proper façade, how deep he'd have to dig to find her again. He was willing to spend some time searching, willing to let her call the shots for the time being, so he'd have the chance.

"Okay. You say when, where, and how. I'll behave myself."

She opened her leather bag and took out a card. She handed it to him. "This is the address and phone number of my gallery. I'm there most of the day. I'd appreciate it if you called me there for now." She looked up at him and grimaced. "I'm not sure how well my daughter will take the news that her mother is *dating*." She got up.

"You don't have to go already, do you?"

She nodded. "I really do. Besides, you're busy." She pointed to the stack of papers on his desk. "Thank you for listening to me."

"Thank you for coming." He didn't try to embrace or kiss her. He only took her hand and squeezed it, then reluctantly let it go. He was at the door, ready to open it so she could leave. "How soon?"

"How soon, what?"

"How soon can I call you?"

She smiled. "As soon as you finish that mound of paperwork. I usually don't leave for home until after nine."

He opened the door and watched until she disappeared into the elevator.

"Brooke, no more interruptions today. No more visitors or phone calls." He went back into his office and closed the door. Then opened it and popped his head back out. "You know, unless it's a matter of life and death. Or it's Mary Claire Beaumont."

Chapter Three

Graham pulled out of the shopping center parking lot and squealed the tires of his new black Mercedes. Three weeks of this goddamn cat and mouse game! He knew he'd told her she could dictate the terms of their relationship, but he was getting tired of it. Tired of meeting her in parking lots and at out-of the-way restaurants. Or worse, her leaving her car in the down-town parking garage so she could meet him at his office. He wanted to pick her up at home, drive her back, walk her to her door, and kiss her goodnight. And then get invited in.

She was killing him. He hadn't been able to do more than take her hand or touch her arm the whole three weeks. He pulled into the lot of a video store. He wanted a movie, something X-rated. No, triple X-rated. Not some piece of fluff that showed a lot of big boobs and nicely rounded butts. He wanted something down and dirty, that showed everything, the secret parts. The parts of a woman you had to work at to see.

He entered the store that, at six o'clock on this Sunday evening, was filled with families; little kids shouting for the latest Disney release and Moms and Dads holding hands and smiling lovingly at their offspring.

Graham made a quick survey of the titles on the shelves and swore under his breath. There was nothing above an R-rating sitting out and the only person working was a sweet faced teenager with long blonde hair. He couldn't very well ask that innocent looking thing to see the *dirty old man* collection in the back room.

Hell, who was he kidding anyway? He turned and left the store. He didn't just want to see any secret parts. He wanted to see her secret parts. Mary Claire Beaumont's secret parts. He wanted to see them and feel them and taste them. And then he wanted to watch her face as he put himself inside her secret parts.

By the time he got to the car, he needed to walk around a little, to let certain things settle down before he could get in. Just thinking of her secret parts did that to him.

Graham thought of the conversation he'd heard in the sauna at the health club the other night. Two guys, about the same age as him or maybe a little older, lamenting the loss of their sexual prowess. It made him happy that he'd taken care of himself. He'd never been a smoker, and although he still had a drink on occasion, he'd given up the asinine, wholesale consumption of alcohol a couple of decades ago, not long after Jamie had been born.

His erection finally subsided enough that he could get into the car. *Damn tight blue jeans.* He turned the key in the ignition and the motor roared to life. At least he was saving money on his energy bill. He wasn't using much hot water these days, not with all the cold showers he'd been taking lately.

A picture flashed in his head. A picture of them together in that tiny little shower stall in Louisville. He'd never known he was a contortionist until then. He remembered the sound of their bodies slapping together and the spray of the water hitting him in the face. Remembered thinking how embarrassing it would be for his family, if he drowned while 'inflagrante delicto'.

He felt himself stir to attention again and scooted around in the seat to relieve the pressure. And then, with apologies to the guys in the sauna, thought, who needs Viagra? I've got Mary Claire Beaumont.

****

Graham was half an hour late making it down the flight of stairs from the penthouse apartment to his office on Monday morning. He was already on his second pot of coffee but he was still in a shitty mood. He'd tossed and turned most of the night, trying to figure out a way to end this stalemate.

He didn't know why Mary Claire was so reticent. Why she so obviously didn't want to be seen with him in places where people knew her. He'd asked her about attending the upcoming Keeneland fall meet with him. She'd used every excuse she could think of to put him off. It wasn't like he was Joe Schmoe boy-toy, or some shyster after her money. But she was still playing some kind of game. He just hadn't figured out what it was yet.

A large mailing tube lay on his desk along with the rest of the day's mail. He set his coffee down and picked up the tube. It was from Hallson, Holderby & King Architects. The drawings for the house renovation.

He spent the next hour pouring over the plans, then had an inspired idea. He picked up the phone and dialed. She answered on the third ring.

"Beaumont Gallery."

"May I speak to the proprietor, please?"

She hesitated. "Graham?"

"Yes."

"May I speak to the proprietor?" She repeated his unusual greeting.

"Well, I thought I should be more formal, since this is a professional call."

"Oh is it?" There was amusement in her tone.

"Yes. I need to engage your services as a sculptor."

"Okay. How may I be of assistance?"

"Umm, you remember the bathtub house?"

She laughed. "Yes, I do."

"Well, I just got the first set of drawings from the architect for the renovations. There are several places inside and a number of places outside where I want to use statuary. I'd like your help in choosing the pieces."

"Well, I'd need to see the plans and the property. In the daylight," she added pointedly.

"Can you get away this afternoon? My schedule is free from one o'clock on."

"Let me see…"

He could hear pages turning, like she was looking at a date book or calendar.

"Okay. Today would be the best day for me."

"Oh, and you may want to wear real clothes. It's still pretty dirty out there."

"Real clothes? As opposed to the fake clothes I usually wear?"

"No. As opposed to those spiffy designer duds you like to sport. I wouldn't want you to ruin your Carolina Herrera."

"You are so considerate. But I just happen to already be dressed in real clothes. I didn't have anyone coming in today and I was planning to be in the workroom all day."

"Okay." He was smiling. "I'll pick you up at one o'clock."

"One-thirty," she said. "I'm having lunch with my daughter."

"One-thirty it is. See you then." He laid the receiver in the cradle.

If he could get her in regular clothes and in sculptor mode, he may just discover his Annabel Lee hiding beneath all that propriety.

****

Mary Claire was enjoying the drive to the *bathtub house*. It was a beautiful October day, warm and bright. When they passed the old, falling down stone gate, she read the carving. "Castleton Downs." She turned to look at him. "Castleton as in Castleton-McCullough?"

"The same."

She was surprised. "I didn't know you had roots in this part of…the country." She caught herself in time. She'd almost said Kentucky.

"Roots, but no ties. I knew the house existed, but I'd never seen it until a few months ago. I bought it when I found out Sean was coming here to live." He glanced over at her. "I thought maybe he'd like to make his home here someday."

"What about you? Are you going to make your home here?"

He didn't answer her right away. Finally he said. "I don't know. That depends on a number of things."

He stopped in front of the house. They got out of the car. He opened the back door and picked up the tube of drawings from the backseat.

Mary Claire was already in professional mode, scanning the area, envisioning how it would look as a finished landscape, and scribbling in her notebook.

Graham pointed with the tube. "I'm thinking I'd like to make the drive circle around, split it down there, just beyond that oak tree and bring it up and around."

"Uh-huh."

"If I do, then I think a fountain, something substantial would look nice here I the middle. What do you think?"

"Maybe a French or an Italian piece?"

"Yes."

"The cost would be…" She stopped, looking for the right word. "Like the piece. Substantial."

He laughed. "It's okay. I can afford it."

"Are you planning a formal garden?"

"Around here." He started around the side of the house.

They spent the next hour walking around the grounds, discussing the merits of a themed landscape as opposed to an eclectic design that looked as though it evolved through the years as the house had. She had six pages of notes by the time they went inside.

"There are several places in here," he turned to look at her, "where I'd like to use some of your work."

"Really?"

"Yes. In the music room. And in here." He led her into a large room that had been a library.

There were still shelves intact, even some books on the ones higher up.

"I'm going to keep this as the library. I thought some of your early literary characters would work well. We could have a couple of lighted alcoves for the stars of the show, and then maybe a few of the smaller pieces, randomly on the shelves."

She surveyed the room. "The alcoves would look nice on either side of the door. Or," she walked over to an expanse of wall, "build this center section in shelving, put an alcove on each side to frame it, and then center your desk in front."

"I can see that. What kind of wood, mahogany, cherry, walnut?"

"It would be nice if you could recreate it as it was." Then she frowned. "That's strange."

"What?"

"Well, this looks like chestnut." She was examining one of the walls that still had shelves. "Wonder why they built all this out of chestnut but used walnut to panel that wall?"

"Don't know. Maybe they just used whatever old trees they had lying around."

"Oh yeah, right." She rolled her eyes.

He extracted the drawings from the tube and spread them out on a make-shift table created from two saw-horses and a piece of plywood. "Ugh, I need my glasses."

Mary Claire was already studying the drawings.

"Why is it you don't need reading glasses? You never put on glasses to read a menu or the newspaper."

"I cheat. I've got contacts that act like bifocals. One eye for close-up one for far away."

"That sounds confusing. I'm ready to capitulate and have laser surgery. I hate having to keep track of those damned glasses. I've got a pair in the car. I'll be right back."

She looked at the drawings a moment longer. This could be a spectacular showplace, and she'd gotten the impression that he was willing to invest enough to make it into just that.

She walked to the window seat beside the fireplace. This was a nice room, spacious, with an excellent view of the grounds. She turned back into the room. The books on those high shelves caught her eye again.

She loved old books. She decided to see what they were. The books were out of her reach. She found a small wooden step-stool that felt sturdy enough for her to stand on. She carried it over and placed it in front of the shelf and then stepped up on it. She stretched. Not quite. She lifted herself up on her tip-toes and stretched again, almost. Her fingers brushed the edge of the binding.

When Graham came back into the room, he saw Mary Claire straining to reach the books. He was above average height, tall really. It was an action as natural to him as breathing. Tall people helped shorter people get things off shelves.

He didn't say anything, he just walked up behind her and reached up over her head with his right hand. Since he was reaching over her, he had to lean in a little to get to the book. When the length of his body came in contact with hers, he automatically wrapped his left arm around her middle and pulled her in to him to steady her. When her derriere made contact with his groin, it caused an immediate reaction.

Her arms quickly dropped to her sides, and he felt her whole body stiffen.

"Oh, god, I'm sorry, Mary Claire. I didn't mean for that to happen." He steeled himself, waiting for the slap he thought was inevitable. But she didn't move. She didn't say anything, and she didn't move a muscle.

His arm still encircled her around the middle. He could feel the quick little in and out spasms of her stomach as her breath caught in her throat. She was crying. He dropped the book onto the floor and put his right hand on her arm, turning her around to face him. Tears were flowing down her cheeks.

"I can't do this anymore."

The breath he'd been holding escaped with a whoosh. *Here it comes.* His face hardened into an unreadable mask. "Can't do what?" His voice was cold.

She grasped both his arms. "I can't be around you every day and keep pretending that it doesn't affect me. Act like my insides aren't doing gymnastics every time I hear your voice. Pretend that I don't care." She hiccupped as a loud sob escaped. "Because I do. I do care, Graham. And I want you to make love to me until I scream and wail and beg for mercy." She reached up and swiped at her eyes, and then looked at him again. "I want you to set me on fire the way you did before."

"I can do that," he whispered, as he leaned his head down and kissed her.

She wrapped her arms around his neck and plastered her body to his.

There was nothing sweet or tender or romantic about this kiss. They tried to devour each other. When they finally came up for air, she gave him a wicked grin and said.

"What'd you do with those mattresses?"

He was already panting. "I had them moved upstairs."

She hopped off the stool. "Let's go." She was unbuttoning as she spoke.

Like the kiss, there was nothing sweet, tender, or romantic about their lovemaking. It was like the movie Graham had wanted to see, down and dirty and hot.

He kissed, nibbled, licked, and probed every square inch of her body and she did the same to him.

He'd waited for her for so long that he was afraid he'd finish too soon. But he needn't have worried. She'd acquired some skills of her own sometime in the past twenty-five years. He gave a fleeting thought to John

Beaumont and wondered if he needed to say a quick thank you. Graham lasted almost an hour before he shot her full of liquid fire and she was screaming and begging for mercy.

"Jesus, bloody hell, woman!" He moaned as he rolled off her.

She didn't say anything but snuggled into the crook of his arm. They lay there with only the ragged sounds of their breathing breaking the silence.

After a few minutes she started talking.

"John was sick for several years before he died. After his first heart attack, I learned some techniques that helped us. After his second heart attack, well, nothing worked." She gave a dry humorless laugh. "He gave me a vibrator for Christmas that year. I used it a couple of times. Then I threw it away. It seemed so horribly sad to me. Besides," and now she squeezed her eyes shut. "I was afraid he'd figure out that I thought the vibrator was more exciting than he'd ever been."

She rolled up on her left side and propped her head up on her hand. With the fingers of her right hand she started drawing circles on his bare chest. "I've been celibate for eight years."

"Completely celibate? Surely you take care of yourself in some way? Even without using a vibrator." He couldn't imagine a creature as sexual as she was with him, not having urges, needs.

"Water." She said.

He frowned. "Excuse me?"

"The bathtub. Shower spray. The handheld one's really nice. It's pleasant, quick. It takes the edge off. And it's not as visceral as a vibrator."

Well, he'd just learned something new. He thought of the shower stall in Louisville again. Of the shower spray hitting him in the face, and then imagined it hitting her somewhere else, on her secret parts.

In one swift motion he rolled to his right, knocking her arm out from under her head and pinning her to the mattress with his body.

She smiled when she saw the expression on his face.

"Would you like another taste?" she teased.

He shook his head. "Not a taste. I want the whole meal." He scooted down so that his mouth was just above the tangle of curly black hair where her legs joined her body.

"Spread 'em," he ordered.

She did. And then squealed with delight as he took his first course.

Chapter Four

Sissy Beaumont was just past eighty. She had snow white hair which she continued to wear in a French twist and clear blue eyes that could look right through you. She still had people come in—to do the cleaning, the landscaping, and the yard work—but the household staff she'd kept in her earlier years had dwindled to one.

Ida Larkin, a widow, was the daughter-in-law of the housekeeper Sissy had hired back in 1945, right after she'd married Jackson Beaumont. Ida, more of a personal assistant than housekeeper, made sure the household ran smoothly. She oversaw all of Sissy's social functions and was as closed mouth as a pit bull with tetanus.

Mary Claire entered the drawing room of Beaumont House on this November day and greeted her mother-in-law who was seated among a display of historic American flags. She looked around the room, then looked at Sissy with raised eyebrows.

"Don't ask." Sissy waved a hand in the air. "It was Laura Ellen's doing. The newspaper people came this morning to take pictures. They're doing a story for Veteran's Day. Seems as though we're the only family known to have an authentic flag from every official military campaign in which the United States has ever been involved. Come on. Let's go in the other room. I keep getting flapped in the face no matter where I sit in here."

They went through the dining room and into the recently added conservatory.

"I just love this space." Sissy sat down in a comfortable high-backed chair. "Wish I'd stood up to Jackson fifty years ago and had it built when I first wanted to."

Mary Claire sat in the matching chair on the other side of the Queen Anne tea table. Ida brought in a tray with a plate of little yellow cakes, two cups, and a pot of decaf coffee. Their luncheon was already on the table. Two plates filled with hot chicken salad, wilted greens, yeast biscuits, and Sissy's famous fruity, creamy, Jell-O concoction. Ida helped Sissy get situated before she left the room.

Sissy gave Mary Claire a quick glance. "Anna Bell's worried about you." She paused for effect. "Says you're acting like a love sick teenager."

Mary Claire bit back a sharp retort.

Sissy smiled and then continued. "I told her to stay out of it. To mind her own business."

Mary Claire looked up in surprise.

"You don't like Anna Bell much, do you?" Sissy spoke softly.

Mary Claire was shocked. "She's my daughter, Sissy. Of course I love her."

Sissy waved a hand in the air. "Oh, I know you love her. I'm talking about like, camaraderie, fellowship, just enjoying each other's company. The two of you have never had that."

Mary Claire lowered her head. "No, we haven't." She paused, then raised her head and looked around the room, like she would find the explanation she was looking for written on the walls. "I don't know. It's like she's never at home anywhere. Almost like she's afraid to get comfortable for fear that someone will send her away." Mary Claire looked at the old woman. "Does that make any sense?"

"It makes perfect sense."

"How is it that she talks to you, Sissy? You've always been the one she runs to."

"I suppose it's because I never had to live in a manner to try and convince her that she's something other than what she is."

Mary Claire wasn't sure she understood that comment.

The conversation lulled while they ate. After a few minutes, Sissy laid her fork down. "So, is this new beau of yours Anna Bell's real daddy?"

Mary Claire choked on the bite of biscuit she was trying to swallow.

Sissy got up and pounded her on the back and then took her seat again when Mary Claire stopped coughing.

"What on earth caused you to say a thing like that?"

Sissy picked up her coffee cup, tilted her head, and looked at Mary Claire until the younger woman dropped her eyes.

"John's been gone for three years now and you've not so much as looked at another man. I figure you must have a history with this one to already be so involved."

Mary Claire tried to think of a plausible denial. She was sure the blank space in her mind was being reflected stupidly in the expression on her face.

Sissy adjusted her position in the chair and then continued.

"Mary Claire, you were a good wife to John. Better than he deserved most of the time. You took care of him and your child. You took care of his house and his business the way he expected. He was my son and like you, with Anna Bell, I loved him dearly. But, darling, he was just like Jackson, dull as dishwater."

Mary Claire looked up and then down at her lap and then up again. "I don't know what to say, Sissy."

"You don't have to say anything. I took care of my family also. I took care of Jackson and this house and his momma and poppa and all the hangers on, but I also took care of myself." She set her cup on the table and leaned back in the chair. "Laura Ellen's daddy was a Swiss banker."

Mary Claire's eyes widened at this revelation.

"I met him on a skiing trip to the Alps. Victoria's daddy was in politics. And well, let's just say Victoria's the reason we ended up with all that Texas oil stock in the Beaumont portfolio."

Mary Claire was speechless.

Sissy smiled. "I've shocked you, haven't I?"

Mary Claire shook her head. "No, not shocked. But I am very, very surprised." She hesitated for a moment and then asked. "Did John know? About Anna Bell, I mean?"

"Oh, I'm sure he did. Most men figure things like that out, sooner or later."

Mary Claire hung her head.

"I always wondered what caused your change of heart. Why you suddenly gave up your dream and rushed home from Louisville ready to get married."

Mary Claire raised her head. There were tears in her eyes.

Sissy's stare didn't move from her daughter-in-law's face. "I don't imagine it took you too long to seal the deal with John when you came back, did it? He'd been pining away for you for months anyway."

"I couldn't find him, the father." Mary Claire spoke quietly. "When I realized that I was going to be alone with a child, I panicked. I didn't have any money. So I

ran home. I didn't want to involve John, Sissy. Really I
didn't. It was Mother's doing. She insisted." Mary Claire
met Sissy's gaze. "John and I had been intimate a couple
of times before. So, no, it didn't take long." She was
quiet for a moment and then said. "You know, he never
asked me about it, about Anna Bell. Not once."

Sissy shrugged. "If you already know the answer,
what good is it to ask the question?"

"I suppose." Mary Claire conceded.

"So maybe that restlessness in Anna Bell is something she can't help. Maybe it's in her blood. Try to talk
to her, Mary Claire. Let her know she's free to roam if
she wants. You know she only stays because she worries
about all of us—you, your momma and daddy, and me."

"I will." Mary Claire looked at Sissy again. "Sissy,
may I tell you something else?"

"Of course."

"I'm pregnant."

"At your age! Well, he must pack an awful powerful
punch. Getting through your protection twice in one
lifetime."

Mary Claire hung her head and flushed red.

"Oh, Mary Claire. You mean he makes you so giddy
you forget to be careful?"

Mary Claire didn't answer.

"Well, I know how that is too. How far along are
you?"

"Just barely. Four weeks."

"Have you seen the doctor yet?"

Mary Claire nodded.

"Is everything all right with the baby?"

"Yes, as far as Dr. Conrad can tell."

"Do you know what you're going to do about it?"

Mary Claire shook her head. "Probably carry it. I wasn't strong enough last time to do anything besides give birth."

Sissy gave her a sharp look. "You think it takes strength to kill a child, Mary Claire? Maybe a temporary surge of false bravado." She turned her head and looked out the window. "Followed by a lifetime of regret." She turned back to look at Mary Claire. "I know."

Mary Claire met the gaze from those piercing blue eyes.

Sissy dropped her gaze then rearranged the bracelet on her wrist. "No, the real test of strength is to do what you did. What I did with Laura Ellen and Victoria. Keep the child and raise it. Provide for it and give the world the opportunity for another Einstein or Beethoven. Or maybe just another someone to run the garden club or play the organ at church."

Tears had started to well up in Mary Claire's eyes again. She tried to stop herself from saying it, but this new found connection with Sissy was too tempting. And she really didn't have anyone else she could tell. "Oh, but Sissy, that's not even the worst of it."

"What do you mean?"

"It's who he is."

"Well, who?"

"Graham McCullough?"

Sissy's face went as pale as her hair. "Oh, dear God in heaven, Mary Claire. What on earth were you thinking?"

"That I'd found the love of my life." Tears were streaming down her face now. "Oh, Sissy, I'm so sorry. I'm so sorry for saying that to you, to John's mother."

Sissy got up from her chair and walked over to stand beside Mary Claire. The old woman patted her back absently. "You mean Anna Bell is…is…?"

Mary Claire's head was bobbing up and down. "Yes."

"Lord have mercy, child." She put her hands on the younger woman's shoulders. "Whatever you decide to do, I'll stand behind you. If you need someone to run interference with Anna Bell or your momma and daddy, let me know."

Mary Claire reached up and put a hand over the one that lay on her shoulder. "Thank you, Sissy. Thank you so much."

They stayed that way for a while longer, until Mary Claire regained her composure. The tender little Madeleine cakes Ida had served them for dessert remained untouched.

At the end of the visit, Sissy accompanied her to the door. "Come visit more often, dear. You don't have to wait until you're summoned."

Mary Claire smiled, leaned over and touched her cheek to Sissy's. "I will."

Sissy watched her down the sidewalk and into her car. The old woman shut the door, then shook her head. "Lord, lord, what a mess!"

Chapter Five

Graham pulled his car into a space directly across the street from Beaumont Gallery and watched as a cold rain pelted the few hardy souls who had ventured downtown on this Saturday morning. The frenzy of Thanksgiving weekend shopping must be taking place at the malls.

He smiled. Life was good. He'd just spent the last few days in Edinburgh with his sister's family. Jamie and Sean had been there too. Graham's family always celebrated the Thanksgiving holiday in deference to their American born mother.

He and Sean had flown back to Lexington together. They'd arrived a little before seven that morning. He'd dropped Sean off at his apartment and then driven out to Castleton Downs. Graham was pleased with the contractor's progress. He couldn't wait for Mary Claire to see how much they'd done since her last visit.

He exited the car, opened his umbrella, and waited for a car to pass before he dashed across the street. He stopped under the shop's awning and shook the water from the umbrella as he closed it. He pulled the gallery door open and went inside. Quiet greeted him. "Oh, Annabel…" he called.

"Yes?" A young woman with long, straight brown hair came into the showroom from the back of the shop. She looked at him expectantly, waiting for him to speak.

Graham was momentarily taken aback. Maybe it was because he'd just spent a week with his sibling, but the girl reminded him of Polly. "I'm sorry. I was looking for Mrs. Beaumont, the owner. She's helping me choose some pieces for a house I'm restoring."

"I'd be happy to look for her notes, if you'd like to see what she's done so far."

"No. That's not necessary. I'll stop by later. Do you know when she'll be back?"

"She won't be back in the gallery until Monday."

"Thank you." He turned and started toward the door.

"Sir."

"Yes." He turned back toward her.

"I'm just curious. If you were looking for my mother, why did you call my name when you came in?"

"Excuse me?"

"When you came in, you called out for Anna Bell."

"Yes."

"That's my name. Anna Bell Beaumont."

His grip on the umbrella handle tightened. "Mary Claire is your mother?"

"Yes."

"And your name is Annabel?" He walked back into the heart of the showroom, closer to her. The resemblance to his sister he'd thought he detected earlier was now like a gong going off in his head. "May I be nosy and ask how old you are?"

She frowned at him.

"I'm sorry, it's just that I have a son who's a student here in his first year at the University of Kentucky, I thought maybe you were a student too."

"No. I've already graduated. I'm twenty-four."

He raised his eyebrows. "Your mother doesn't look old enough to have a twenty-four year old daughter." He took a deep breath. He felt like someone had just kicked him in the stomach. "I have a hobby. I like to try and guess people's birthstones. May I try to guess yours?"

"That's different."

She worried her bottom lip with her upper teeth in a gesture so like Polly that he actually felt a physical pain shoot through him.

"Sure go ahead."

"It's akin to guessing someone's astrological sign, only harder. You know, because the way star signs span more than one month." *God, where had that come from?*

He stared at her face, the slant at the corner of her mouth, the color of her hair, and the shape of her hands, until he could tell she was becoming uncomfortable.

"Garnet?" He was certain his guess was wrong.

"No, but close. You're one month off. It's amethyst. I was born in February, not January."

"Ah, well, as you can see, I need more practice. I'm not very good at this hobby."

She was smiling. "If you leave your name, I'll be sure to tell Mother you stopped."

"No, that's okay. I'll just drop by next week."

He left the shop, crossing the street in the now pouring rain, the closed umbrella still clutched in his right hand.

He started the car and wiped the water dripping onto his face from his rain soaked hair. He sat there breathing deeply, trying to calm himself. Damn her! How could she not tell him? He picked up his cell phone and hit the button for Brooke's home number.

"Hello."

"Brooke, this is Graham McCullough."

"Oh, yes sir."

"I really hate to call you at home and on a holiday weekend, but I need a street address. Last name Beaumont. B-e-a-u-m-o-n-t. First name John."

Brooke called him back in a matter of minutes and gave him two addresses. There was no listing for John Beaumont, but there were two for J. Beaumont. There was no one home at the first one. He pulled into the circle drive of the second. The plaque on the brick gateway had proclaimed this to be Beaumont House.

His knock was answered by a sixty-ish looking lady in a navy pants suit.

"Hello. My name is Graham McCullough. I'd like to see Mrs. Beaumont, if possible." He handed her his business card.

The woman moved aside so he could enter. "Step in, if you will, and I'll see if Mrs. Beaumont is receiving visitors this morning."

"Thank you." He paced up and down the entry hall, examining the photographs and paintings as he waited.

In a few minutes the lady reappeared. "Mr. McCullough, if you'll come this way please." She led him through the dining room and into the conservatory.

An elderly woman with white hair stood to greet him.

"Mr. McCullough, please come in. I'm Sissy Beaumont."

"Thank you for seeing me. I apologize for stopping by unannounced."

"Not at all. Please have a seat." She indicated the high back chairs that were her favorite. "What can I do for you?"

"I'm looking for Mrs. Mary Claire Beaumont."

"Oh?" Sissy's eyes widened as she looked at him. "Mary Claire is my daughter-in-law but she doesn't live here."

"Yes, I know, but I hoped you might know where I could find her today. I've already been by her business and her home and she isn't at either place." He drummed his fingers on the arm of the chair.

Sissy stared pointedly at his hand and then moved her gaze to his face.

He stopped the motion of his hand in mid-air.

"Well, I imagine Mary Claire is at her momma and daddy's today, helping with the decorating. Her momma always hosts Christmas open house the first week of December for the officers of the garden clubs from all around the state. They normally start decorating on the Saturday after Thanksgiving."

"Oh, can you tell me how to find her parents' home?"

"No." Sissy shook her head. "I don't think it would be a good idea."

He scooted out to sit on the edge of the chair. "Mrs. Beaumont, it is very important that I talk with her today. I beg of you to reconsider." He started drumming his fingers again.

"No, Mr. McCullough. I don't think it would be at all wise of me to send you straight into the midst of a whole gaggle of Rutherfords, being as how you're already in a greatly agitated state." She motioned toward his drumming fingers.

"Rutherfords?" The question dropped from his mouth like a stone.

"Yes. Mary Claire's family. She was Mary Claire Rutherford before she married my son."

He slumped back in the chair. "Well, that explains a lot."

Sissy gave him a moment before she spoke. "You said you'd been by the gallery. I take it you've finally met Anna Bell?"

He looked at her but didn't say anything.

"Mr. McCullough?"

"Yes. Yes, I did."

"Try not to judge Mary Claire too harshly, Mr. McCullough. She really does care for you a great deal."

"Oh, yes." His tone dripped with sarcasm. "She's made that perfectly clear."

When she spoke again, Sissy's tone was like steel grating on steel. "Mr. McCullough, I'd advise you to tread lightly in your dealing with my daughter-in-law. And especially where Anna Bell is concerned. You see, technically, she may not be of my blood. But she's been my granddaughter since the day she was born. I trust you'll keep that in mind."

He looked at the dead calm that was set in her ice-blue gaze. Damn it! Had this old woman just threatened him? He got up from the chair. "Mrs. Beaumont, I assure you, the last thing I want is to have anything to do with the Rutherfords. Any of them. Thank you for your time. I'll show myself out."

Chapter Six

Mary Claire sat at her drawing table. She sipped on her pomegranate fizz as she made sketches for a new statue. This concoction of 7UP and pomegranate juice was the one thing she'd found that could settle her stomach.

She tapped her pencil on the drawing table and glanced at the phone. It was Thursday already and she still hadn't heard from Graham. She knew he was back. Anna Bell had casually mentioned his visit to the shop this past Saturday. It had to have been him. His was the only project Mary Claire was working on right now. So why hadn't he stopped back or called her?

She heard the buzzer that indicated the front door had opened. She got off the stool and went out to greet her customer. Mary Claire was pleasantly surprised when she saw Sissy standing in the showroom. Sissy never came downtown anymore.

Sissy looked around and smiled when Mary Claire entered the showroom. "This is nice, Mary Claire. You've done a fine job here. Very subdued and dripping with elegance. You should have done it years ago."

Mary Claire walked over to Sissy and gave her a quick hug in greeting. "What brings you downtown, Sissy?"

"I came to see you. I'm afraid you're going to be unhappy with me, and I wanted to get it over with. Out of the way."

"Come sit." Mary Claire led the way to a small alcove off to the side of the main display area. It was the place her clients could sit and look through the catalogs of her work or describe to her what they wanted as she took notes. "May I offer you something to drink?"

Sissy shook her head. "Nothing you're serving these days." She looked around the space. "You know, this building used to house a rather upscale little night spot just after the war. Jackson and I frequented it on occasion."

"Why do you think I'm going to be upset with you?"

Sissy looked at her and then said. "Graham McCullough paid me a visit Saturday."

Mary Claire's eyes widened. "Why?"

"He was looking for you. I told him where you were."

Mary Claire's posture stiffened. "He didn't come to Rutherford Commons."

"I didn't expect he would. He said he'd already been here and by your house and since you weren't at either place, he tried my home."

"How'd he know where you live? I've never even told him where I live."

Sissy gave her a patronizing look. "Mary Claire, the man runs a multi-billion dollar company. I don't expect it's difficult for him to find an address in a city this size."

"I guess not."

"He was very agitated when he came to see me, Mary Claire and very insistent that he needed to talk to you immediately."

"Well, that doesn't make sense. I haven't talked to him, Sissy. Not since the Sunday before Thanksgiving. If he was so anxious to talk to me why hasn't he called or come in again?"

"That's part of why I think you're going to be upset with me. Not only did I spill the beans about your being a Rutherford, but I told him to think long and hard before he said or did anything where you were concerned. And especially where Anna Bell was concerned."

Mary Claire sucked in her breath. "But Sissy, he doesn't know about Anna Bell."

"Mary Claire, why do you think he was looking for you? He'd already been in here and seen Anna Bell."

"But he just saw her."

"And talked to her and found out she was your daughter. Anna Bell doesn't look like him, but she doesn't look like you either. For a fact, she doesn't look like anyone on either side of your family. Don't you think it stands to reason that she may resemble someone in his family?"

"Oh, God." Mary Claire groaned.

"He as much as admitted to me that's why he wanted to talk to you."

Mary Claire was glad she hadn't eaten today. She would have thrown-up if she had. "He must despise me." She slumped back into her chair.

"No." Sissy countered. "What I saw was a wounded man. I'm sure he feels hurt and ill-used. But make no mistake, there's still passion there."

"Hatred takes passion too, Sissy."

"He doesn't hate you, Mary Claire. Even if he's angry and mad as hell at you right now. He doesn't hate you."

Mary Claire felt as limp as a dishrag. All the strength drained right out of her.

"You say he hasn't called you?"

"No, he hasn't."

"Well, the thing is, I think I may have intimidated him just a bit. He may be waiting for you to contact him."

Mary Claire sat up straight. "I can't do that. What would I say?"

Sissy pulled herself up into a posture of authority. "You will do it. Or are you so fond of being miserable that you'd choose to spend the rest of your life that way too?" Sissy's voice softened as she continued. "Think of the child you're carrying and think of Anna Bell, if not yourself. Don't you think she deserves a chance to get to know him, to have a relationship with him? She won't, you know, if you're not on good terms with him. She's that loyal to you."

Mary Claire's eyes were bright with tears when she looked at Sissy again. "I guess it can't be any worse than when I came home and faced my mother and father the first time I was pregnant."

Sissy got up and started for the door. "Does he even know about this new baby?"

"No."

Sissy turned just before she went out. "Sounds as though you have more than enough to warrant a phone call to Mr. McCullough."

****

Mary Claire waited until the next day. She didn't call him. She went to his office to see him in person. She waited until five minutes before it was time for Brooke to go home. Mary Claire knew Brooke would let her go in to his office without announcing her. She also knew that Graham wouldn't make a scene or be awful to her while Brooke was still there. And five minutes was enough time for her to determine whether she had a chance to make amends or if all was lost.

She opened the door to his office and stepped in. She'd made a hasty change into what he would call *real clothes* before she'd left the gallery. An outfit she'd picked up at Tommy Bahama. Nice, but it didn't scream designer label like most of her wardrobe.

He glanced up and then gave her a look that felt like a knife plunging into the depths of her soul.

"What do you want, Miss Rutherford?"

He said the name with such contempt that she felt the imaginary knife twist.

"We need to talk," she said with a cheerfulness that sounded hollow even to her own ears.

"Why?" He jerked the reading glasses off his face. "Why talk now? You've managed not to say anything for twenty-five years. Why break your record?"

"Damn you." Her hands clenched into fists at her sides. "Goddamn you and your self-righteous indignation." She had an awareness that this wasn't in the script she had prepared, but she couldn't stop. "Who in the hell are you to judge me? You're the one who disappeared off the face of the earth. I tried to find you. If that lame ass company of yours had kept any kind of records, you'd be able to check. Four months, Graham. Four solid months I tried." Tears welled up in her eyes. "So long that when I finally went to the clinic it was too late. I didn't have any choice then."

She was crying now, tears of anger and frustration, tears of sadness. "So I came home, Mr. McCullough. I came home and gave Clay Rutherford a grandchild. A grandchild that my mother insisted was to be a Beaumont. Daddy didn't care if the baby was a Beaumont or a nobody. But he would sure as hell have cared if he'd ever known Anna Bell was a McCullough."

She flung her head back and snuffed loudly. "And oh, God," she groaned. "I wasn't strong enough to fight that battle alone. So I did what my mother wanted. I seduced poor John and then left him to wonder for the rest of his life when Anna Bell showed up way too early." Mary Claire slumped to her knees and sat there huddled on the floor, sobbing.

Graham got up from his chair. He knelt on the floor in front of her. His eyes were also bright with tears. "I was in South America. My father's expedition had gone missing. I spent six months in the jungles of the Amazon basin looking for him, for any trace that he might still be alive. I didn't find him."

Mary Claire raised her arms up and held on to him.

"I came back, Mary Claire. I stopped in Louisville before I even went back to Edinburgh. I looked everywhere for you. But I didn't know your name."

She sobbed even louder.

"I made one last trip looking for you, three weeks before I married Barbara." Tears trickled down his cheeks as he slid his arms around her waist. "Mary Claire." His voice was a whisper. "My Annabel Lee, marry me now. I'll be your champion. I'll fight any battle you want." He paused for a moment and then said. "Just please don't ever ask me to go one-on-one with Sissy Beaumont."

Mary Claire shrieked and then laughed uncontrollably.

Graham laughed too and then started kissing the side of her face and neck. "Will you?"

She pulled away from him and looked at his face. "I need to tell you something else."

"What? What other secrets could you possibly need to impart?"

She lowered her eyes and swallowed hard then looked up at him. "I'm pregnant again."

He surprised her. He smiled from ear to ear. "Then you'll have to marry me." He pulled her close and hugged her. He kissed the top of her head and rocked her from side to side. "You can't be very far along."

"Seven weeks."

He put his hands under her sweater and skimmed them up her back and then down again. He moved them to the front of her body and cupped her breasts. "Do you feel like making love?"

His voice was like a soft caress that touched her whole body at once.

"Yes."

He pulled the cushions off the sofa and the chair and also took the seat cushions fro the two wing chairs. He arranged them on the floor into a make-shift bed, then laid her back onto it.

Their lovemaking was sweet, gentle, and slow. He pulled her sweater off over her head and then unfastened her bra. He laid the items of clothing aside and lowered his head to her. He ran his tongue around the circle of her nipples and then nipped softly and suckled gently at each one. She moaned in delight.

He unbuttoned the band at the top of her slacks and unzipped them only enough to let his hand slide inside them. She wasn't wearing panties.

"Going commando today, are we?" He raised his eyebrows.

"I was in a hurry when I changed clothes. I didn't know anyone was going to check."

He slid his hand further and dipped his fingers into the moisture of her private places. He slid his middle finger deeper causing her to arch her body up, against his hand. He drew his hand out of her slacks and put his fingers in his mouth, tasting her sweetness.

Watching him caused her to flood with moisture again. "Graham please." She begged.

"What?" He unzipped her slacks all the way this time.

"Inside me. I want you inside me, now."

He shook his head. "Not yet."

She wiggled out of her slacks while he stripped off his own shirt and stood up and kicked off his shoes. He unfastened his trousers and let them drop to the floor and stepped out of them.

"Come here." She motioned for him to kneel again.

He did.

She ran her hand up the leg of his boxer shorts and took hold of his erection. Of the solid, overtly male feel of him. She pulled slowly, in the motion he had shown her he liked, all those years ago.

"You have an excellent memory, my Annabel Lee."

"Now," she said again.

He shook his head no a second time. He let himself enjoy the movement of her hand a few seconds longer and then stilled her motion and moved her hand from his body. He stood up and removed his shorts.

He lay down beside her and started stroking her, making sure to bring a portion of the moisture up from her depths with each stroke as his hand slid across her. She was writhing. After a few minutes, he poised himself over her and ever so slowly, slid himself inside her.

She wrapped her legs around him and tried to force him to increase the speed of his thrusts.

He didn't. He kept it slow and steady and even. And then he rolled off and lay beside her again and brought her to climax with his hand. Spasms still wracked her body when he filled her with his flesh a second time and found his own release in the sweet madness of rebirth.

Chapter Seven

Clay Rutherford hated the Christmas season. It wasn't so much Christmas he hated. It was all them damn parties Caroline expected him to go to. They weren't even a whole week into December and they'd already been to three. A man couldn't even set home and watch a ballgame anymore, not in the whole month of December!

They'd gone to the Country Club party Saturday night. It wasn't too bad. At least there you could sneak off to the men's locker room and grab a smoke if you wanted.

But he'd been trying for two days to come up with a reason Caroline would buy as to why he couldn't go to this one tonight. The Museum Holiday fundraiser would be politically correct out the wazoo. And he did hate politically correct. No way he'd be able to sneak a smoke there. Hank's phone call had come just in the nick of time.

Clay walked in the house and started up the stairs. He made sure to change the expression on his face from a big smile to a look of resigned regret before he entered the bedroom where Caroline was already getting dressed.

"Henry Clay Rutherford, where have you been? You need to hurry up and get showered. I laid out your clothes already." Caroline was digging through her jewelry box.

"Caroline, I just talked to Ben. He's coming to escort you to the Museum party."

She stopped digging in her jewelry box and turned to face him with her hands on her hips. "What?"

He nodded his head. "Hank called from the barn a little while ago. That mare we bred to SunKing is having some trouble. Hank thinks we need to stay with her tonight."

"That is why you pay an exorbitant sum of money to keep a veterinarian on staff. He and Hank can handle the horses."

Clay was shaking his head. "Not tonight. That mare herself if worth a couple hundred thousand. If this foal is a colt he could bring over a million at the next sale. I think I'd rather be in the barn tonight. Hell, even if I was at the party I wouldn't do anything but worry about it all evening anyway. I wouldn't be any fun and then you'd be mad at me."

"I'm mad at you now." She turned away from him.

"I know, but if you go with Ben you'll have a good time and get over being mad at me by the time you get home. You may have such a good time that I could even get lucky tonight!" He moved his eyebrows up and down, teasing her then reached over and pinched her on the behind.

She slapped his hand away. "Don't count on it." She started digging in her jewelry box again. "I told Richard Townsend you'd be there. I know he wants to talk with you about the new wing."

"Caroline, he don't give a rat's ass on my opinion about the new wing. He just wants my money. Write them an extra big check tonight. They won't care if I'm there or not."

She sat down in front of the mirror on her dressing table to put on the pearl earrings she'd taken from her jewelry box.

He watched her from where he sat on the bed. "Is Anna Bell going to be there tonight?"

She fastened one earring and then shook her head. "No, she went to some function in Cincinnati. She won't be home until late tonight. I swear, Clay, I just know she's going to end up moving away. She's always off somewhere else, and she isn't involved with these local events nearly as much as she should be."

He shrugged.

Caroline fastened the other earring. "Maybe I should ask Sissy to speak to her about it. Lord knows it won't do any good to ask Mary Claire to talk to her."

Clay chuckled. "Guess I don't even have to ask if Mary Claire will be there. I tried to set her up with a date. That fellow that just started last month over at the Red Mile." Clay was shaking his head. "But of course she didn't want anything to do with him. You know, it wouldn't hurt her to help me out a little. You never know when a contact like that could come in handy."

"Why is it you only try to use Mary Claire as a pawn?" Caroline's voice held a note of disapproval. "Why aren't you arranging liaisons for Ben now that he and Pam are divorced?"

"Not the same. Not many suitable single women that high up in the businesses I need contacts with."

"Well, I think you should stop it. Leave Mary Claire alone. Besides, don't you think she's already done her penance?" Caroline looked at him in the mirror.

"What the hell does that mean?"

"I mean she stayed married to John Beaumont for over twenty years." Caroline turned around on the stool to face him. "Having John Beaumont for a son-in-law didn't hurt when it came to your business dealings. I seem to remember you taking advantage of that connection quite often."

"That's what families do for each other. Help out. Why'd you call it penance?"

She turned back to the mirror and picked up her hairbrush to smooth some fly-away strands. "I don't know." She sighed. "I don't think Mary Claire was happy, in a personal sense. I don't think their love life was very exciting."

"Well, she sure as hell must have liked it before the wedding. I mean, correct me if my memory fails, but wasn't that love life what caused her to have to marry him in the first place?"

Caroline dropped her eyes. "You're being vulgar."

"You brought it up."

She applied her lipstick and then dropped the tube into the beaded handbag that was lying on the dressing table. She checked her reflection one last time and then got up.

Clay stood up and walked over to the window that looked out on the front of the property. "Ben's coming up the drive now. You have a good time tonight."

****

Ben Rutherford pulled on his trousers and then tucked his shirt tail in before he fastened them. He put on his shoes, then picked up his jacket, tie and belt and headed downstairs. He'd shower and shave and put on fresh clothes when he got to the office.

He hadn't planned on staying all night in his old room, but he did need to talk to his dad about two deals they had on the table right now. Besides there was no way he was going to miss seeing the old man's face when he found out.

Dad and Hank must have spent the entire night in the barn. Ben hadn't heard any explosions coming from his parents' room in the overnight hours.

Ben made his way to the kitchen. Hank was already sitting at the table eating. He definitely looked like he'd spent the night bedded down with the horses. "Is Dad still in the barn?"

Hank shook his head. "No. He came in sometime around two this morning. She'd made it past the crisis point by then. Looks like she and the foal are going to make it okay."

Ben was frowning as he poured himself a cup of coffee and then sat down at the table.

"Didn't know you were staying last night." Hank stabbed his fork into a pile of grits on his plate.

"Hadn't really planned on it. But I need to ask Dad about a couple of things. And evidently tell him something too."

"What?" Hank asked around the fork full of grits he'd just stuck in his mouth.

Ben didn't answer.

Just then Clay came into the kitchen. He went to the counter and poured himself a cup of coffee then picked up a plate and filled it with the food the cook had left on the stove.

"Well, it's been a while since the two of you have been here for breakfast at the same time." Clay sat down and started eating.

When Ben asked, Clay offered his opinion of the business deals Ben had questions about. Then the three of them discussed which of the horses they'd likely sell off in the coming year. Clay and Hank finished eating and were sipping their coffee.

"So," Ben leaned back in his chair. "Mom tell you about the show you missed last night?"

Clay shook his head. "She was asleep when I got to the bed. She's still asleep. What show?"

"The one your daughter put on?"

Clay frowned. "At the Museum party?"

Ben nodded.

"Mary Claire was there?"

Ben nodded again.

"She come by herself?"

This time Ben shook his head. "Oh no. Not by herself." He sat his cup down, scooted to perch himself on the edge of his chair, folded his arms and rested his elbows on the table. "She was there with her new fiancée and sporting a four carat diamond on her left hand."

Hank perked up. "Do what?"

"What in the hell are you talking about, fiancée?" Clay growled. "She ain't even dating anyone."

"Well she may not be dating, but she's sure as hell doing something." Ben was enjoying the reaction. "I've never seen her look so happy."

"Well who is he?" Hank asked.

"Now that's the interesting part." Ben was prolonging the news as much as he could. "Seems as though he's a newcomer to the horse industry. A Scot, by the name of Graham McCullough!"

Chapter Eight

Sissy was seated at the antique writing desk in the sitting area of her bedroom suite. Still in her dressing gown, she was looking through the stack of cards and invitations Ida had brought up yesterday. Sissy had already missed four events that she personally considered important but never attended. She was steadfast in her rule. Someone had to be. No Christmas parties before the tenth of December. If someone didn't put a stop to the nonsense, they'd start scheduling holiday parties right after Labor Day.

She was considering which of the invitations she might accept when she heard a commotion from downstairs.

She walked out of the room to the stair landing overlooking the front hall. Anna Bell stood in the hall with Ida. The girl was practically wailing.

"What's wrong, child?" Sissy called down to her.

Anna Bell looked up and then ran up the stairs. "Oh, Grandmother, it's just awful. I don't know what to do." She threw herself into Sissy's embrace.

Sissy patted the back of the girl's head, like she had when Anna Bell was a child. "Ida, go ahead and bring us some breakfast up here. And some coffee. The real stuff. And, you might want to add a splash of bourbon to mine."

She led Anna Bell into the sitting room, then guided her to the loveseat and sat down. "Now what has you so upset today? Did someone tell you there's no Santa Claus?" Sissy tried to cajole her granddaughter.

Anna Bell ignored the comment. "Oh, Grandmother. It's Grandpop Rutherford and Mother. They had a just awful fight."

"When?"

"This morning. Mother and I both got in really late last night and we were still asleep when we heard a terrible pounding on the door. When Mother opened the door, it was Grandpop. He was all red and screaming and they said just horrible things to each other. He said not to bother coming for Christmas because she wasn't welcome in his house ever again."

"Oh dear." Sissy was shaking her head.

"And then Mother called him a sanctimonious, controlling old bastard and said she didn't care if she ever saw him again. And…" Anna Bell looked at Sissy's sympathetic expression and started sobbing again.

Sissy wrapped the girl in her arms and let her cry for a few minutes before she decided on her course of action. It always amazed Sissy, the depth of affection she felt for Anna Bell. Her love for this one was stronger than for any of Laura Ellen's or Victoria's children. Maybe it was because she'd always known that Anna Bell would need her the most.

"Anna Bell." Sissy's voice was firm. "Sit up here now and listen to me." Sissy pulled a tissue from the box that sat on the table next to her and handed it to Anna Bell.

Anna Bell wiped her eyes and blew her nose and then did as her grandmother asked.

"Anna Bell, you're not a child any longer. For a fact, you're a very beautiful woman. And I know you've had some experience in matters of the heart," Sissy gave her a knowing look, "and matters of the flesh."

"Grandmother!" Anna Bell blushed. "What does that have to do with anything?"

"Because this whole mess, this disagreement between your mother and your grandpop is because of just such matters."

A tap sounded at the door.

"Come in." Sissy called.

Ida brought in the coffee service and a small cruet filled with an amber colored liquid. She set it on the tea table and then went back into the hallway and re-entered with a tray that held muffins, fruit and yogurt.

"Thank you, Ida. I think we'll be a while yet."

Ida nodded and left the room.

Sissy poured two cups of coffee and then sweetened her cup with the bourbon. She took a sip before she started talking again. "Jackson and I always maintained a cordial relationship with Caroline and Clay Rutherford. The whole time our children were in school together. Through the years when John and your mother dated. When she ran off to Louisville and didn't want anything to do with him, and then when she came back and they took up again. And all through the years of John and Mary Claire's marriage."

Sissy took another sip of her coffee. "When Jackson died, Clay and Caroline were as good as gold to me. And since John's death they've been even kinder." She sat the coffee cup down. "Anna Bell, sometimes people do things for reasons we don't know about. Sometimes what looks to be a perfectly normal situation is anything but." Sissy shook her head. "The things we do for God, country, and family."

"Grandmother, I don't understand anything you're saying."

"Let me tell you about my family." Sissy patted Anna Bell's leg. "My mother and father came to the United States as newly-weds, just after the First World War. My daddy had been a baker in France. And by the time I was born he had found work in a little bakery here in town. I was the oldest of five children and even though Daddy's work was steady, it didn't go a long way in supporting such a large family. We were poor as church mice. I didn't have anything except an undocumented family history that said we were sprung from the nobility even though most of those ancestors had parted ways with their heads during the Terror."

"The Terror? Are you talking about the French Revolution?"

Sissy nodded. "I could still carry a title if I wanted." She picked up her cup and took another sip. "The Beaumonts were also French. But they were Huguenots. They'd been here for more than two hundred years by the time my family came. They'd settled in this part of the country when Kentucky was still a part of the Virginia Commonwealth."

She sat the cup down and leaned back on the loveseat. "Everyone loved Daddy's breads and pastries. Jackson's mother was overly fond of the baked goods." Sissy grimaced. "She was of a portly stature. She used to hire my daddy, after hours, to come and bake for her social functions. I sometimes helped him."

"Jackson's daddy ran the tobacco exchange, the market where they auctioned off the burley. He was also a stockholder in several banks and had some railroad holdings. Jackson had taken a liking to me when I'd help Daddy bake for the parties. His daddy was opposed to the match because we were Catholic and poor. But his momma argued that we had aristocratic blood and if I'd just promise to quit going to church she thought it'd be fine."

"Your family was Catholic?"

"We were indeed."

"I had no idea." Anna Bell picked up the cup of coffee Sissy had poured for her earlier.

Sissy kept going. "I knew that Daddy was sick and that my mother and my three sisters and my brother would be destitute if he died. So, I put away my rosary beads and took down my crucifix. I married Jackson Beaumont and became a part-time Presbyterian. I married Jackson to save my family. Just like Mary Claire married my son to save her family."

"What are you talking about? Mother didn't need Daddy's money. Grandpop has money out the wazoo and always has." Anna Bell sat her cup on the table.

Sissy smiled, hearing Anna Bell use Clay's famous verbiage. "Not from financial ruin, darling. From social ruin." Sissy took Anna Bell's hand in hers and patted it with her other one. The she reached up and cupped the young woman's chin and gave her a loving smile. "You were already on the way when Mary Claire came home from Louisville."

Anna Bell made a gesture of dismissal. "It was the seventies, Grandmother. Those things happened."

"Yes they did."

"But I still don't understand. They got married so what was the problem?"

"The problem was that Mary Claire never had any intention of marrying John. She would have married your real father, but she couldn't find him. He was out of the country. She couldn't get in touch with him to tell him about you. She thought he'd abandoned her."

Anna Bell inhaled sharply. "Are you saying Daddy wasn't my father?"

Sissy nodded.

"And she lied to him and married him anyway! And let him think, and let me think…" Anna Bell drew her left hand from Sissy's grasp and covered her mouth with it. Her right arm was across her stomach. She was rocking back and forth on the loveseat. She moved her hand away from her mouth.

"How could she? How could she do something so awful?"

"Awful? Anna Bell!" Sissy's voice commanded obedience. "Look at me."

She did.

"Your mother did what she had to do. What your grandmom, Caroline insisted she do. Mary Claire came home, young, pregnant, and heart-broken. Caroline is a Southern Baptist through and through. She was already incensed over Ben's unsuitable marriage. Adding an illegitimate grandchild to the mix was not a humiliation she was willing to accept."

"But it was all a lie."

"And who did it hurt? Your mother was good to John. I couldn't have chosen a better wife for him. Think on it yourself. Did you suffer while you were growing up? Did your daddy? No. John was happy. He'd always loved Mary Claire and he loved you, as do I."

Anna Bell hung her head.

"No, the only person who ever suffered for it was Mary Claire." Sissy patted Anna Bell's hand again.

They sat in silence for two full minutes while Anna Bell digested the information.

"But then what happened now to make Grandpop so angry?"

"Well, the annual Museum fund raiser party was last night."

"Yes, mother actually went."

"You know how tongues wag at those things. I imagine Clay found out who your real daddy is."

"Grandmother, I 'm not following your logic. Why on earth would that subject come up now if it hasn't for the past twenty-five years?"

"Because he's here, in Lexington."

"You know who he is?"

"Yes. He paid me a visit just after Thanksgiving. You've met him too, Anna Bell."

"I... I..." She sucked in her breath. "The man who came into the gallery, looking for Mother?"

"Yes. He told me he'd been by the gallery and met you."

"No wonder he kept looking at me so." She was quiet for a moment. "What's his name? He didn't tell me his name."

"It's Graham. Graham McCullough."

"McCullough! Oh no, not the ones Grandpop hates?"

Sissy nodded. "The same. Thus the conundrum."

Anna Bell leaned over and laid her head on Sissy's shoulder.

"Anna Bell, if your grandpop should act differently toward you, try to understand. Give him some time to work through his hurt and feeling of betrayal. He loves you, darling. He'll get back to being your grandpop." Sissy put her arm around Anna Bell's shoulder. "Now, weren't you planning on taking a little trip this week? To New York City, wasn't it?"

Anna Bell nodded. "But I can't go now."

"Of course you can." Sissy got up and went to her desk. She took out her checkbook and scribbled for a minute. She tore the piece of paper from the book and handed it to Anna Bell. "Here. Treat your friends. Stay an extra day and go shopping."

Anna Bell looked at the figure on the check. "Grandmother!"

Sissy waved a hand in the air. "It's only money, child. Now you go on and have a good time. And, leave this business to me."

Anna Bell hugged her grandmother. "I love you."

"I love you too, baby."

Sissy walked downstairs with Anna Bell. She accepted the girl's kiss on her cheek. "Don't worry, Anna Bell. It'll be fine."

When Anna Bell's car pulled out of the driveway, Sissy called for Ida. She was halfway up the stairs when Ida came into the hall.

"Ida, give me a few minutes to get dressed and then bring the car around. We're going to pay a visit to the Rutherfords. I've had enough of this nonsense."

****

What actually happened that Tuesday morning in the front parlor of the main house at Rutherford Commons was never known by anyone except the three players in the drama.

Caroline Rutherford would rather have had her tongue ripped out than confide her humiliation to anyone. Clay Rutherford was never going to admit he'd been cowed by a woman, even if it was Sissy Beaumont. And Sissy herself wasn't about to reveal the secrets to the source of the power she wielded.

But whatever had transpired, when Sissy made her way down the front steps and toward the car, headed home, she was satisfied that the outward displays had been put to rest. She hoped Clay and Caroline had the good sense to bury the demons that caused the rift, not just shut them up in the closet again to let them fester and then escape in another ten years. No, she wanted it over and done. She wanted Anna Bell to be happy. And Sissy really didn't think Clay was foolish enough to defy her in this. He had that much sense anyway.

Clay Rutherford stood at the parlor window and watched the straight, stiff set of Sissy Beaumont's back as she made her way down the walk.

He'd heard the stories for years, knew Sissy could carry a big stick. But he'd never worried about it. After all, he and Caroline were family. They'd always been on good terms with Sissy. He watched as she climbed into the passenger side of the silver gray Mercedes sedan.

"Caroline," Clay turned toward his wife, "that woman is the devil incarnate."

Caroline was on the sofa, her handkerchief held to her face, sniffling. She didn't give any indication that she'd even heard her husband's comment, but only said, "Shall I call Mary Claire or will you?"

Chapter Nine

Christmas Day at Rutherford Commons was more subdued than usual. Caroline did her best imitation of the long-suffering, put upon martyr. Clay allowed Mary Claire in the house, but he didn't talk to her at all. Anna Bell chattered incessantly and tried to pretend that all was well.

Ben brought his new, much younger girlfriend of two weeks—whom Clay kept calling Pam—and her two, not very well behaved young children. Ben's son and his fiancée were there, but Ben's daughter was with the real Pam. Hank and his wife, Michelle were the only ones who seemed like they were really having a merry Christmas.

They ate dinner at three o'clock and opened gifts afterwards. By six o'clock even Hank and Michelle were eager to escape. Mary Claire was the first to bolt.

"Anna Bell, you about ready to go?"

Anna Bell nodded and had her coat on in record time. They said their goodbyes and gathered up their gifts and loaded into Anna Bell's Christmas gift from Sissy, a bright red Hummer. They had celebrated at Beaumont House on Christmas Eve.

"Well, that was about the worst Christmas ever." Anna Bell said as they pulled away from the festively lit façade of Rutherford Commons.

Mary Claire started laughing. "It was pretty bad, but not the worst I've witnessed in that house."

"You're kidding, right" I can't fathom anything worse."

"Oh no, not kidding at all. You should have been there the first year Ben brought Pam home. Every place setting on the table had a miniature crèche in the middle of the plate. Daddy said a dinner blessing that went on for ten minutes and then made us sit through a reading of the whole Christmas story from Luke before we got to open gifts. Which just all happened to be wrapped in baby Jesus paper."

"Grandpop being holier than thou." Anna Bell laughed. "Now that's a good one."

"He surely was. Though it might have played better if he'd actually gone to church with us that morning." Mary Claire gazed out the window enjoying the Christmas lights along the way. "What are you going to do this evening?"

"I thought I'd stop by Grandmother's."

"Oh? I figured Sissy would be out and about tonight."

"No. Aunt Vickie and her bunch are still there. And Aunt Laura said Michael and Macy aren't leaving until tomorrow."

"Well at least you'll have a good time there. Maybe it will make up for the Christmas dinner from hell we just left." Mary Claire paused for a moment and then said. "You know you're welcome to come with me."

Anna Bell kept her eyes trained forward. "I know, Mother. It's just that… I just can't. Not yet."

Mary Claire reached over and patted her daughter on the leg. "I understand."

Anna Bell helped Mary Claire take their gifts inside and then left for Sissy's.

Mary Claire went upstairs. She undressed and climbed into the shower. She still had an hour to get ready. Graham wasn't picking her up until eight o'clock. She luxuriated in the warm spray caressing her body. She moved her hands to her stomach and smiled.

She must be crazy. She was forty-five years old and she wanted this child like she'd never wanted anything before in her life. Maybe she saw it as a chance to redeem the mistakes she'd made with Anna Bell. Maybe it was knowing that she and Graham would raise this one together. Whatever the reason, she didn't care. She was happy. Sissy had been right. Mary Claire was so used to being miserable that she'd never even realized she was until Sissy had pointed it out.

She got out of the shower and dressed in soft merino wool slacks and a matching cashmere tunic sweater in winter white. Chic, but very comfortable. She'd dusted her face with powder and put on some eye shadow and mascara and just a hint of lipstick. Her hair she'd given a quick twist and fastened with a sparkly clasp that hopefully would hold until Graham took it out to let her hair fall free. She smiled. Just before he divested her of her clothing. For some reason Graham seemed to like her with frizzy wisps. John had preferred the more sophisticated sleek, slicked down look. But then, John had like everything orderly. From the very beginning, even their sex life had been scheduled.

But in a way, so was hers and Graham's. It was scheduled for every time they were alone together for twenty minutes.

Mary Claire looked around the room she'd shared with John. She wondered if Anna Bell would want this house. Mary Claire would move in with Graham as soon as they were married. First, into the penthouse apartment, then into Castleton Downs when the work there was finished.

In a way Mary Claire hoped Anna Bell would keep the house. It was good to have roots, to have a history. Anna Bell had that, even if it was a fictionalized version.

Chapter Ten

January 2004

Mary Claire considered Graham's question and finished spreading the mound of straw before she answered. "I don't care where we get married." She moved out of the stall. "Let me rephrase that. I do care. It's just that I don't need a whole crowd of people to be there. A nice private little ceremony with just the two of us is fine with me. I'd prefer it really."

She and Graham were working in the barn at Castleton Downs preparing it for the first of the horses that would be shipped the following week. The barns and workers' cottages had been the first priority in refurbishing the farm.

Hamish wanted to get the horses moved and settled in before the spring racing schedule started. He'd had the workers fix up the old barns to use while the new, state-of-the-art ones were under construction a little further down the lane.

Graham walked up behind her and wrapped his arms around her. "Well, if you want to get married in a church, it'll have to be yours."

She twisted her head around to look at him. "Duh! We are in Lexington, not Edinburgh."

He shook his head. "No, I mean Presbyterian or Baptist or whatever you are."

This time she turned all the way around to face him. "Why? I mean, what church do you go to?"

"Catholic."

She was surprised. It had never occurred to her that he would be something other than Presbyterian. "I thought the whole of Scotland was Presbyterian."

"Sorry, but no."

"They teach us here that everyone in Scotland has a secret statue of John Calvin stashed away." She was smiling. "Hey, that could be my next project. Millions of little pocket size John Calvin statues for the Scottish market. They could be key chains."

Graham laughed. "You're being very silly."

"I know. I like being silly. I don't do it nearly often enough."

Graham walked over to the flatbed wagon, hoisted another bale of straw and carried it into the next stall. He cut the bailing string and went back to get another.

Mary Claire carried her pitch fork in and began scattering the straw across the floor. "Seriously, though, why couldn't we get married Catholic, if we wanted?"

"Because, my dear, my marriage to Barbara has never been annulled. According to Church Law she is still my wife until they say otherwise."

"Well that's stupid." It was all she could think of to say.

"It doesn't matter. A ceremony somewhere with a judge is fine with me."

"Me too. I don't have anyone I particularly want to ask to stand up with me anyway." She turned and lifted another forkful of straw from the bale. "I don't think Anna Bell will even come."

"Oh."

Mary Claire heard the disappointment in his voice. She stopped spreading the straw and looked at him. "What?"

"It's…I just thought maybe…oh never mind." He smiled and walked over to the wagon for another bale.

She followed him. "Tell me what you were going to say."

"I just thought the music room here, you know, the bathtub room, is almost finished. I though it would be nice to get married in there, and maybe have Anna Bell and Sean be our witnesses."

That's a beautiful sentiment. And it would be wonderful. But I honestly don't think she'll come." Mary Claire walked to the next stall.

"Does she really hate me?" He asked.

"No, not you. Her problem is with me." She leaned the pitch fork against the side of the stall.

"But you said she's coming around?"

"She is. But I think it's going to take more than a month for her to really forgive me." Mary Claire had tears in her eyes. "Graham, she's moving away." She said it quietly and then the tears started flowing down her cheeks. "She's accepted a position in California."

He walked over and wrapped his arms around her.

"My baby is leaving." Mary Claire sobbed.

"She is nearly twenty-five years old, Mary Claire."

"I know." She leaned back and looked at him. "At least she's not leaving until after her birthday. Sissy's throwing her a big party."

"She would, wouldn't she." He looked around the barn, at what they'd accomplished on this Sunday afternoon. "Why don't we sit down for a while? You must be getting tired."

"I could stand a breather."

They walked over and sat down on the part of the flatbed wagon that was cleared.

"So how many horses is Hamish bringing this trip?"

"Two three-year olds, a brood mare, a colt and that big Scottish stud." He looked at her and grinned.

She leaned against him like she was swooning. "But darling, I thought he was already here."

Chapter Eleven

February

The big Scottish stud was in a really bad temper. He'd already kicked the side out of two stalls and was doing his best to do the same with a third. He'd also tried to bite the younger horses earlier. Mary Claire thought he just didn't want to be close to any of them.

She sighed. "I'll just move him to that stall at the far end away from the others. I'm sure glad Hamish moved the mare to the other barn before he left."

Graham swore. "I don't know why he had to take everyone with him." Graham's mood was beginning to rival that of the horse.

"They went after six horses. It takes a few people to handle a job like that." She looked over at Graham and smiled, trying to calm him down. "They'll be back tomorrow, probably by midmorning."

Graham's hands-on experience with horses was minimal. Working in the barns was something new to him, but it was old hat to Mary Claire. She had grown up in the barns at Rutherford Commons.

She walked toward the big horse's stall. "We'll just get him settled down, and it'll be fine."

The stallion let loose with another kick to the side of the stall.

"Mary Claire, no." Graham followed behind her. "I'll move him."

She shook her head. "You've already moved him three times. You're as mad as he is." She took a lead from the hook on the outside of the stall. "You'll just upset him more."

She opened the gate and walked into the cubicle. The big horse eyed her warily. She crooned and coed to him and reached her hand out. It took a few seconds, but he finally dipped his head and nuzzled her hand. She reached up and patted his nose.

"That's right, big fellow. We're going to be friends." Her voice was soft and calming. She reached up and grasped his bridle and fastened the lead to it, then led the horse out of the stall and into the one at the far end of the barn. When she unsnapped the lead from the bridle, he gave a little jerk and bumped against the gate causing a curry brush to fall to the floor.

Maybe it was all those years of living with neat freak, John that caused her to do it. Maybe it was because she hadn't been with a horse this wild in a long time and had forgotten, or maybe it was fate.

The horse was almost all the way into the stall, when Mary Claire stepped behind him and bent down to pick up the curry brush. He gave a mighty kick with his hind legs and caught her square in the stomach as she was straightening up. The kick sent her flying across the center aisle of the barn and into the wall on the other side.

****

Clay and Caroline Rutherford were standing at the door waiting to get on the elevator as Sissy got off. A curt nod was the only greeting Clay offered. He stepped past Sissy into the conveyance.

Sissy reached out her hand to take told of Caroline's outstretched one. "How is she, Caroline?"

"They had to give her two more units of blood around sunrise, before they finally got the bleeding stopped. But they say she's going to be fine."

"What about the baby?" Sissy asked quietly.

Caroline squeezed her eyes shut and shook her head.

"Caroline! I can't hold this elevator forever." Clay's brusque voice came from inside the car.

Sissy let go of Caroline's hand and started down the corridor.

Mary Claire was in a private room at the end of the hall with it's own waiting room. Graham was sitting there alone when Sissy walked in. He'd apparently been here all night. He was still dressed in jeans, flannel shirt, and work boots. His eyes were red-rimmed and his face was darkened with two days growth of a beard.

Sissy sat down beside him. "Mr. McCullough, let me express my deepest sympathy. I am so very sorry for your loss."

He swallowed hard and struggled to gain control of his emotions before he spoke. "Thank you."

"I know how much Mary Claire was looking forward to this child. I am profoundly sorry." Sissy pointed toward the door to Mary Claire's room. "Is she asleep?"

"No. Anna Bell's in there with her right now. She went in when Mr. and Mrs. Rut...when Mary Claire's parents left."

Sissy sat there with him. She didn't say anything but only reached over and took his hand when she saw the tears leak from the corners of his eyes.

"I shouldn't have let her do it. I should have insisted. She shouldn't have even been out there, close to that horse. But she's always so damned confident, thinks she can do anything."

"It was a freak accident, Mr. McCullough. It wasn't your fault."

"Thank you. Thank you for your kind words." Then he gave a dry humorless snort. "You know, you're the first person today to acknowledge I even exist."

"I know the Rutherfords and the McCulloughs have hated each other for several generations. Do you know why that is?"

"No, not really. I do know my grandfather did everything he could to throw a monkey wrench into any deal he thought might remotely have a positive impact on the American burley or coal market. He knew the Rutherfords held large interests in both." Graham gave Sissy a wry smile then shook his head. "He fancied Turkish cigarettes and promoted the merits of Welsh coal to all his associates. My own father wasn't so rigid. I guess he was more Billenshire than McCullough."

"Billenshire?"

"Yes, my grandmother's family."

"And Anna Bell told me the Rutherfords and the McCulloughs were distant relatives."

Graham nodded. "The Castleton family. Two sisters, one married to a McCullough and the other married to a Rutherford."

"How very interesting." Sissy turned toward the door to Mary Claire's room as Anna Bell emerged into the waiting area. She got up to hug her granddaughter.

"Mother said she heard your voice. She wants to see you."

"Will you be here when I come back out?"

Anna Bell glanced at Graham. "No. I'm going to run home and get her toiletries and some clothes for her to wear home. They said she could leave in the morning, if everything goes okay until then."

Anna Bell gave Sissy a quick kiss on the cheek. "I'll see you later." She left without acknowledging Graham at all.

Sissy raised her eyebrows. "How about you, Mr. McCullough? Will you be here for a while?"

He rubbed a hand across the stubble on his chin. "Unless they make me go home and take a shower."

Sissy waited for the door to close behind her before she walked to the bedside. She patted Mary Claire's hand then sat down in the chair beside the bed. "Anna Bell said they're already saying you can go home?"

"Yes. I just have to stay in bed for two weeks."

"Well, do you want to come to my house? Let Ida and me look after you?"

"No. Anna Bell will be with me."

"She will? I thought she was supposed to leave Wednesday."

Mary Claire moved her head slowly from side the side. "She called and talked to them this morning. She was able to switch starting dates with another girl who was supposed to start in May."

"I see."

Mary Claire closed her eyes. A sob caught in her throat. "Oh Sissy, I wanted this baby so much."

"I know you did." Sissy stood up and patted the sheets that covered Mary Claire.

Mary Claire grabbed Sissy's hand and looked up at the old woman. "I think I'm being punished."

"Punished? What are you talking about?"

"I think I'm being punished for wanting it so much. Punished because I never really wanted Anna Bell." She snuffed and wiped her hand across her eyes. "I mean, it was so stupid. I knew better. I worked in the barns the whole time I was growing up. I know you don't step behind a horse that's already in an agitated condition. Especially one that big." She was still crying. "How will he ever forgive me?"

"How will who forgive you?"

"Graham. He was as excited about the baby as I was." Mary Claire wiped her eyes with a tissue this time. "I seem to have a very bad habit of denying Mr. McCullough of his offspring."

"Oh God, Mary Claire, you nearly died! I'm sure he doesn't think it's a Rutherford conspiracy. The man truly loves you."

Mary Claire squeezed her eyes shut and nodded.

"And don't forget, Mary Claire. Your body has suffered the trauma, but he's suffering too. He's lost a child the same as you have."

"I know." She turned her face away from Sissy and gazed out the window. "And it's all my fault."

Chapter Twelve

March

The sun was disappearing behind the line of trees on the north-west horizon of Castleton Downs, leaving the roadway from the barns to the house in shadow and causing the air to chill. Graham stuck his hands in his pockets. He needed to shower and change clothes before he went to visit Mary Claire.

He should have stopped this afternoon on his way from the airport. He clenched his teeth together just thinking about it. He'd never been such a coward before. He hated to admit it, but he'd enjoyed being away for the last two weeks. Away from the scathing looks he got from Anna Bell each time she opened the door and said, "Oh, it's you." Like she'd rather invite Satan into her home rather than the sperm donor who was her father.

He wasn't sure what he would encounter tonight when he visited. He'd called Mary Claire every day while he'd been in London, but he hadn't talked to her since Tuesday, five days ago. The excuses were different each day, and at first he thought Anna Bell was just being contrary and not letting him talk to her mother. But yesterday, he'd heard something else in Anna Bell's voice. She sounded apologetic, almost sympathetic, when she's told him Mary Claire was indisposed and wasn't able to speak with him right then. She'd even sounded— well *nice,* when he voiced his concern for Mary Claire's health and insisted on knowing if she'd had a set back.

Anna Bell assured him that the doctor had given Mary Claire a good report after her examination on Friday.

So if it wasn't Anna Bell, then why wouldn't Mary Claire talk to him? His insides twisted. He knew. Deep inside he knew. She blamed him for the accident, for the death of their child.

God knows he blamed himself. He'd played it over and over again in his mind. Why on earth had he let her near that goddamned horse?

Graham was almost to the house when he heard a car coming up the drive. He stopped and waited until it came into view. It was Mary Claire's Lexus. His heart started thumping in his chest. He walked to the side terrace and waited until she pulled up. He felt a shiver go through him. She was alone. No Anna Bell, no Sissy, no one but her. She had come to see him, alone.

He smiled as he opened the driver's side door and held his hand out to help her from the car. She hesitated before she took it. She was painfully thin and there were dark circles beneath her eyes, but she was still the most beautiful woman he'd ever laid eyes on. He wrapped his arms around her.

"It's good to see you out. Come on, let's go inside."

She pulled away from him and shook her head. "If you don't mind, I'd rather stay out here."

He frowned at her.

"I've been cooped up inside for too long."

"You're sure?"

She nodded.

"It's not too cold?"

"No." Her voice was barely audible.

He looked around and then remembered the newly finished low stone wall across the back of the rear terrace. "We can sit back there." He pointed toward the corner of the house.

He took her arm and led her to the wall that would eventually serve to divide the terrace from the yet-to-be-installed swimming pool. She lowered herself slowly to sit on the cold stone. They sat side-by-side in the encroaching darkness.

Silence.

He watched as she twirled the loose fitting diamond ring around the fourth finger of her left hand.

"Sissy said you sold the horse."

He shook his head. "Hamish sold the horse. I wanted to shoot it."

They were quiet again.

"I was worried about you this week."

She turned her head to look at him.

"I was afraid you'd taken a turn for the worse, when I didn't get to talk to you."

"Is that why you didn't stop this afternoon? Because you were so worried about me?" Her voice was like ice.

He felt his gut twist. "No, Mary Claire. I mean, Anna Bell assured me you were doing fine. I was on my way inside right now to get cleaned up, so I could come visit."

She turned her face away from him.

He could feel it coming. Feel it in the clipped way the words dropped from her mouth. In the way she held herself, stiff, not letting her hand or leg touch his. He dropped head and closed his eyes. He opened them again just in time to see her stop twirling the ring and slide it off her finger.

"Mary Claire?"

"Graham, I...this isn't..." Her head moved from side to side. "I can't..." She got up, folded her arms across her stomach, and looked toward the barns.

His chest felt like it was being squeezed in a vice. He couldn't do this again, lose her. She was as vital to him as air, water, and food. He wanted to take hold of her and shake her. Make her stop what she was about to do. Make her understand that it was a mistake. He wanted to beg her forgiveness, tell her he'd make it all okay. That he'd protect her and keep her safe. But she knew as well as he what a lie that was. He'd promised to be her champion, to fight her battles, but had let her walk full force into harm's way while he stood by and watched.

So instead of doing anything, he sat there and waited.

She turned to face him and held her closed hand toward him. "I think it's better if you take this back."

His throat was as dry as if he'd spent a week in the Sahara. He swallowed hard. "Mary Claire, if you need some time, I understand." He stood up. A scant three inches separated them but it may as well have been the Grand Canyon.

She leaned her head back and looked at his face. Her expression as cold as her voice had been earlier. "I don't need any more time, Graham." She bent and laid the ring on the stone wall and started toward her car.

He wanted to go after her, wanted to make her listen to reason, any reason. Even though there was no reason. He'd abandoned her the first time and had stood idly by as she walked into danger the second. His guilt, like lead shoes stopped him from moving, rooting him to the spot where he stood.

He heard her car door shut, heard the engine rev, heard the tires crunch on the gravel as she drove out of his life. He picked up the ring and closed his hand around it. The point of the marquis cut dug into his flesh as both his hands clenched into fists. He felt the pain as the stone broke his skin. And then he felt the pain that welled up inside him, building until it consumed his whole being. Until he thought he would surely die of it. He drew his hand back and threw the ring as far as he could.

Mary Claire got to the tumbled down stone gate before she had to stop the car. The road shimmered and swam before her. She grabbed a tissue from her pocket and held it to her face in a futile attempt to dry the tears that streamed down her face.

She was right. His feeble attempt to stop her had been a pretense. She was sure all he felt right now was relief. Relief that he didn't have to be the one to end it. Relief that he never again had to look at the woman who'd stolen one of his children away from him and caused the death of another.

She shut the motor off and sat there in the darkness, her sobs drowning out the sounds of the croaking frogs. The sounds that signaled the arrival of spring, the return of life to the land. The sounds that mocked her very existence.

Chapter Thirteen

April

Sissy hung up the phone and opened the top drawer of the desk. She wished Adeline Montgomery would just go ahead and quit. She fished in the drawer until she found the list of substitute players. It was Sissy's turn to host the bridge club today. Adeline always had some crisis looming, but they never occurred early enough for her to find her own substitute. No, that always fell to whomever was hosting that particular day.

Sissy scanned down the page. One name caught her eye. He wasn't the first in the order she should have called, but if he was able to come, she just might be able to kill two birds with one stone today. She dialed the number for the rectory at Saint Mark's Cathedral.

"Saint Mark's. This is Father Pat."

"Father, this is Sissy Beaumont."

"Hello, Sissy. What can I do for you?"

"Well, we need a fourth for bridge today. Can you make it?"

"I have to say Mass at noon. What time are you starting?"

"Play will start at three o'clock, but I was hoping you could get here about one-thirty or quarter of two. I'd like to talk to you about something."

"At your house?"

"Yes, Father."

"Don't see why I couldn't."

"That would be wonderful. And don't worry about getting something to eat. I'll feed you here."

"Okay, Sissy. I'll see you this afternoon."

She hung up the phone and smiled then went to the closet in her sewing room and dug out the box that had been buried in the back for decades.

****

Anna Bell took her grandmother shopping. Sissy bought a new dress, new shoes, a hat, purse, and a pair of white gloves. And on Easter Sunday morning Anna Bell drove her grandmother to church.

Graham McCullough stood outside Saint Mark's waiting for Sean. Graham hadn't been to Mass since he'd come to Kentucky, but there was just something about not going to church on Easter.

He'd even be able to receive communion today if he wanted. He'd gone to confession for the first time in eons, right after the…the incident. A pang of melancholy shot through him. And God knew that, other than a few venial sins, since then he was on the path of the straight and narrow. He closed his eyes and thought of how much he missed Mary Claire.

"Good morning." Sean's voice came from behind Graham.

Graham opened his eyes and turned around to face his son. "Good morning." He gave Sean a hug. "Let's go in."

The church was nearly half full already. Graham was sure it would be packed today. The overflow caused by those like him who only showed up for the biggies, Easter and Christmas. He was trying to decide where they should sit when he spotted an outrageous hat. He was pointing it out to Sean when the lady wearing it turned her head. It was Sissy Beaumont.

Sean still hadn't spotted it.

"Come on. You can see it when I introduce you to the lady."

Graham didn't see Anna Bell until he'd already committed himself. To change course now would draw more attention than just going on with it. Sissy's head was turned toward Anna Bell. Graham touched Sissy on the shoulder as he spoke.

"May we join you?"

Sissy looked up with surprise. "Of course."

"Sean, this is Mrs. Sissy Beaumont and…and her granddaughter, Anna Bell Beaumont. Ladies, this is my son, Sean McCullough."

Sean was staring at Anna Bell.

Anna Bell turned her head away from them and scooted further into the pew so they could sit down. Graham slid in beside Sissy and Sean sat by the aisle.

"I'm please to meet you, Sean." Sissy smiled and then looked at Graham. "Mr. McCullough, I didn't realize that you were of the Roman faith."

He nodded. "There are still some Catholics in Scotland. A few made it out of Culloden to procreate," he said as he and Sean knelt to say their devotion.

****

"Mr. McCullough, I hear you've done wonderful things with Castleton Downs." Sissy returned several nods of greeting as they exited the church.

"It's turning out well."

"But you're still leaving us?"

"I'll be back in Edinburgh by the end of the month." He confirmed.

"Surely you can't mean to miss the Derby?"

Graham nodded. "I'm afraid so. My associate, Hamish MacDougal will be there. But yes, I'll miss it." He held his arm out to Sissy. "May we see you to your automobile?"

She took his arm and pointed. "We're in that monstrosity of Anna Bell's."

"Grandmother, you're the one who bought it."

Sissy looked at Graham, raised her eyebrows, and shrugged. "It's still a monstrosity."

He patted her gloved hand and laughed.

They were standing beside the Hummer. Anna Bell brought the set of miniature steps from the back seat that Sissy used to climb in and out of the vehicle.

"Mr. McCullough, don't stay away. You were like a breath of fresh air to the community. You're welcome in my world anytime." Sissy gave Anna Bell a pointed stare as she spoke.

"Thank you, Mrs. Beaumont. It has been my great pleasure to make your acquaintance. I hope I may call you friend?"

"But of course." Sissy turned to Sean. "Young man, if you ever need anything while you're here, please feel free to call on me." Graham helped her into the vehicle.

Anna Bell started to reach for the step but Graham beat her to it. Her hand brushed his in the attempt. She pulled her hand away and walked around to the driver's side. He followed, carrying the step. She opened the back door and he placed the step in the floor of the back seat. She moved in front of him to reposition it before she closed the door, so that the step sat squarely on the towel she'd laid on top of the carpet.

Graham took her by surprise when she turned back around. He leaned in and gave her a quick kiss on the cheek.

"Goodbye, baby," he whispered.

Anna Bell raised her hand to the spot where his lips touched her as he walked away.

Chapter Fourteen

Sissy sat motionless. "Mary Claire, how much longer is this going to take?"

"Sissy you can move. You're not sitting for a portrait. I'm only doing sketches to supplement the photographs."

Mary Claire was doing a bust of the old woman. The museum board had been after Sissy for years to have it done. They wanted it for the director's room, since Sissy was the most generous benefactor they'd ever had. Sissy had been difficult to convince. "I'd rather have been immortalized as a sweet young thing. Not a crotchety old octogenarian," she'd said.

Mary Claire had agreed. "Then I'll work off photographs. I'll make you ageless. You'll be like the Venus DeMilo or Nefertiti."

Mary Claire had spent her whole married life trying to avoid her mother-in-law. But since that November day when Sissy had summoned her to lunch, four years ago, they'd come to be very close friends.

"Sissy, may I ask you something?"

"Of course. Don't mean I'll answer, but you can ask."

"You very well may not."

Mary Claire added a few more lines to her sketchpad. "Anna Bell said you told her once that you married Jackson for money. And you told me yourself about Laura Ellen and Vickie. Tell me the rest of it."

"I don't know what you're talking about, the rest of it." Sissy turned her head and raised her hand to study her manicure.

Mary Claire stopped drawing. "Sissy, I've gotten to know you very well over these past few years. And whether the reason you married Jackson was for his money or not, you had a husband. You were bound to him by the laws of God and man. That's not something you'd dismiss lightly."

Sissy looked around the expanse of the conservatory and then smiled. "Right before I started attending Mass at Saint Mark's, I sat in this very room with Father Pat and made my confession. He was the first person I ever told the whole story to." She looked Mary Claire directly in the eye. "I guess you'll be the last."

"Meaning what?"

"Meaning that it's no one else's business. No one else needs to know any of it."

"I will protect your story with my life." Mary Claire made the mark of an X across her chest. "Cross my heart and hope to die."

"I hope you mean d-y-e, not d-i-e."

"That would be more appropriate these days, wouldn't it?" She ran a hand along the top of her dark hair where strands of silver were beginning to show.

"Oh, I don't think being gray is a handicap." Sissy patted the sides of her up-do. "This snow cap only adds to the mystique." She tilted her head and stared at Mary Claire. "The part of the story I told Anna Bell, I told her because I wanted her to understand why you married John. I wanted her to know that we're all capable of doing things for the benefit of those we love that may seem despicable to others."

"Thank you."

"I did marry Jackson for money. I married him to save my family from a life of poverty and despair. It wasn't until a few years later that I found out what I'd signed on for. Why his mother was so willing to let him marry a Catholic girl from a family with less than nothing."

Sissy got up from the chair and stretched. She walked to the window and looked out. "Seems as though I was the first girl Jackson had ever shown any interest in." She turned back toward Mary Claire. "Any interest at all." She chuckled. "You know how women these days are always saying they want to be appreciated for their minds? Well, let me tell you, it's not all that flattering. Especially when you're young and pretty and ready to experience life. Jackson was interested in me because I could carry on an intelligent conversation and I could make him laugh. Physically, he was interested in other men."

Mary Claire gasped. "Oh, dear God, Sissy. I would never have guessed in a million years."

"He hid it well." Sissy sat back down. "At first, I tried everything I knew of. I thought I was deficient in some way. Because the only way Jackson could tolerate me was to be drunk. And let me tell you, there's a fine line between being drunk enough for a homosexual to have intercourse with a woman and being so drunk that he couldn't have sex with anything."

"Sissy, I'm sorry. I had no idea. If you'd rather not say anymore, I understand."

"I don't mind telling you, Mary Claire. We were in New York at some social function at the home of one of Jackson's business associates. He had disappeared and I didn't know a soul there. I went looking for him. I found him in one of the upstairs bedrooms." She squeezed her eyes shut and then opened them again. "I was in a state, let me tell you."

Sissy picked up a framed photograph of John, Laura Ellen and Victoria off the side table. She looked at it as she continued. "I was sick, disgusted, horrified, but in another sense strangely relieved. Relieved to know that it wasn't me."

She sat the photograph back on the table. "I ran down the stairs and literally straight into the arms of a man I'd met once before on a previous trip. He'd been watching me all evening. I don't know if he knew about Jackson or if he just thought I was attractive. But he took me back to our hotel and he stayed for a while trying to comfort me. I'd been married for almost three years and until that night, the closest I'd come to making love was when Jackson had a wet dream. Funny, I can't even remember what the man looked like.

Sissy got up again and walked to the window. "I ended up pregnant, scared to death. I didn't tell anyone, but I fretted about it until I made myself sick. I went to see old Dr. Rawlings. He was a man of science, didn't give a tinker's damn for religion. He took care of my problem for me." Sissy crossed her arms over her stomach. "I'd already turned my back on my faith and committed adultery, so how much hotter could hell be? I thought I could do it and never look back. But I was wrong."

She stopped talking. Mary Claire thought she had finished her story, but she started again.

"I can't tell you how many times I've longed for that child through the years. I thought about drinking myself into a stupor or going back to see Dr. Rawlings, to see if he'd give me some tranquilizers. And then one day, I just decided that I was better than that. That the best thing I could do was live. Really live. That the best form of penance I could pay would be to continue to do what I'd already done. Spend my life helping and making it easier for the people I love. Come here, Mary Claire."

Mary Claire walked to the window to stand beside her.

"See that obelisk out there?"

"Yes."

"It's not just a garden ornament. I had it put up as a memorial to the child whose life I took away. Through the years when things were difficult or I felt overwhelmed, I go out there and sit, draw strength from it, and renew my commitment to the pledge I'd made to myself."

Sissy walked to the sofa and sat down. "I redoubled my effort with Jackson and finally, after seven years, managed to get pregnant. Lord, Jackson's momma and daddy were so happy when John was born, you'd have thought I'd given them the crown prince." She sighed. "I though having John would be enough to keep me happy. And he was for a few years. But I really wanted more children."

Mary Claire pickup her sketchbook out of the chair and sat back down.

"I told Jackson I intended to have more children." Sissy laughed. "He said he didn't care as long as he didn't have to provide them. So I told him I'd conduct my private life in a discreet manner, if he'd do the same and never, ever question the paternity of my future children. They were to be Beaumonts. No ifs, ands, or buts. And that's how we left it. Jackson and I were roommates and social partners, nothing more, for the rest of our marriage."

"You are an amazing woman." Mary Claire's voice held a not of awe as she spoke.

"No, Mary Claire. I only did what I thought I had to do. Just as you did."

Sissy was quiet for a while as Mary Claire made a few more sketches. Then she asked. "Do you ever hear from Mr. McCullough?"

Mary Claire shook her head but didn't look up.

"Damn fool nonsense, if you ask me. Someone should have slapped some sense into both of you."

Finally, Mary Claire did look up. "Sissy!"

This time Sissy's voice was soft. "It just breaks my heart, Mary Claire. The two of you belong together. And for some reason, the two of you seem to be the only ones who can't figure that out."

"Well, I appreciate the sentiment, but it's over and done with. He's gone and this time, he's not coming back."

"Did you ever really talk about it?"

"What, Sissy? That I destroyed his life again? That I gave him hope for a future with a real family life and then shattered it, killed it right in front of him? Is that what you want to know if we talked about?" Her eyes glittered with tears.

Sissy exhaled loudly. "He blamed himself, you know. Said you'd never forgive him for not insisting he take care of that horse."

"Well that's silly."

"My point exactly." Sissy leaned back on the sofa. "Both of you blamed yourself and were so sure that the other must feel the same way that you never even said that to each other."

Mary Claire flung her head back and shook it wildly. "It doesn't matter anymore, Sissy. It's over. Now may we please get this finished?"

Sissy frowned and was quiet again for a minute before she said, "Well, what do you know about this young man Anna Bell's seeing?"

Chapter Fifteen

July 2011

Mary Claire stashed her overnight bag on the floor of the back seat and hung her dress on the bar above the door. She draped the skirt across the seat and hoped it didn't get too wrinkled. She climbed into the driver's seat of her new Cadillac Escalade and checked again to make sure she had everything she was supposed to take.

At first, she'd been a little hurt when Anna Bell had said, "I'm getting married and all you have to do is buy a nice dress and show up." Mary Claire knew it couldn't be that easy. Then Anna Bell had thrown in the catch. "I want to use Castleton Downs for the event."

It made sense. After all, Castleton Downs was truly Anna Bell's legacy. The ancestral home of both sides of her family. Her blood family, that was.

Anna Bell had gone on to say that Sissy was paying for everything and it wasn't like she was a twenty-year-old who wanted some fairy tale wedding with a big poufy gown and a hundred attendants. She said there wasn't even all that much to do. Just order a few flowers and hire a caterer and a band. They weren't even going to have a rehearsal, since it was only them and two attendants. And Uncle Hank had agreed to make sure the house was ready, if Mary Claire would just say yes. So she had.

Anna Bell's young man, as Sissy always called him, was a thirty-five year old divorced father of two. Brian Kemme had grown up in Fort Thomas, Kentucky, across the river from Cincinnati, Ohio, though he and Anna Bell hadn't met until they were both working in California.

Mary Claire marveled at how much Anna Bell had changed since she had gone to work for Kentucky Spirits as an account executive for European imports. Her job required extensive travel across the United States as well as Europe. Her little girl had turned into a poised and polished professional woman.

She wondered how well Anna Bell would cope with the role of step-mother. Mary Claire had her doubts, but she kept her concerns to herself. Brian's children lived with their mother in Sacramento and since he and Anna Bell traveled so much, their contact with the children would be minimal.

Mary Claire turned off the highway and gasped. A few flowers indeed! The drive leading into Castleton Downs looked like it had been ground zero for a hydrangea bomb. She was sure Anna Bell and Sissy must have caused a world-wide shortage of the blooms after adorning this venue. Ropes of greenery, flowers, and tulle draped along the fence on both sides of the road, punctuated about every twenty-five feet with groupings of potted ferns and hydrangeas. The whole scene was gorgeous.

Mary Claire hadn't been out here since the night she'd given her engagement ring back to Graham. He'd gone on with the renovations. Hamish had overseen the job after Graham had moved back to Scotland.

Then he'd made that one trip back and insisted on seeing her. They'd met at her attorney's office. He'd set up some kind of fund for Anna Bell—like she needed it. But he'd insisted.

And then he'd brought up the subject of Castleton Downs. It was all done, Graham had told her, except the library. He was leaving that for her to complete.

Despite her vehement protests, he'd signed the property over to her and left. The house had just been sitting empty ever since.

Hank had aggravated her so about letting the new state-of-the-art barns and stables sit empty until she had finally relented and let him manage their use. Mary Claire smiled. He was using some of them for Rutherford Commons horses. The rest he was renting out. At least he was making enough that the property wasn't costing her anything in upkeep or utilities.

Her heart caught in her throat as she pulled up to the formal entrance of the property. The drive had been widened to easily accommodate the side-by-side passage of three modern vehicles. The original stonework had been rebuilt and new construction to match it extended some fifty feet on each side until it met a stand of oaks and poplars on the left and joined the white rail fencing on the right.

The new entryway, a solid surround built of limestone with wrought iron gates across the opening, reminded her of the Arc de Triomphe. Rectangular lampposts joined the main structure to the original stonework. On the right upright of the limestone structure was carved a single word—*McCullough*. Exactly opposite it, on the left side, was etched the word—*Rutherford*, and across the top lintel, *Castleton Downs*. Incorporated into the iron work of the custom made gate was scrolled *Bountiful Bluegrass*.

The lamps on each side sat atop replicas of Mary Claire's own interpretation of Pegasus, done oh so many years ago. She had to sit there for a moment. Her insides were already in turmoil. And now to see this, completely unexpectedly, nearly undid her.

It was five hours until the scheduled time for the wedding to begin so the gates were still closed. She dug in her purse and found the slip of paper where she'd written the security code for the gate. She punched the number into the keypad. The wrought iron gates slowly swung open. The drive split just on the far side of the gate, winding through the grounds on its circular approach to the front of the house.

He had made some other changes since she'd last seen the plans. The fountain she had suggested was there, but instead of being in front, it had become the centerpiece of a gigantic reflecting pool that itself had water jets in alternating heights surrounding the antique piece. The whole of it being the focal point of the vista that stretched to the south, a flowing carpet of lawn that opened up behind the grove of oaks and poplars she had driven along-side coming in.

The north side of the house was a blur of activity. There were two catering vans still unloading as well as a florist's truck and the musicians' van.

Mary Claire was driving slowly on her approach to the house, watching the comings and goings. She was almost directly in front of the entry before she really looked at it. She stepped on the brakes and then sat there staring. Where in the world had he found them? She didn't even know what had happened to them.

Flanking the front door of the mansion were the life size statues she'd done of Romeo and Juliet during the Shakespeare period of her literary phase. The same Juliet that Graham had fondled that night in her art studio. Dear God, she was never going to make it through this day.

Her head jerked around as someone tapped on the driver's side window. The valet moved back when she opened the door.

"Oh, Mrs. Beaumont, I didn't realize it was you. You got a new ride."

"Jimmy? Is that you?" She hardly recognized him in his valet uniform.

"Yes, ma'am."

"Where are you working now? I haven't seen you at Rutherford Commons for a while."

"Here." He pointed toward the barns. "Mr. Hank moved a bunch of us over here last fall."

"Oh, well, it's good to see you again." She handed him the keys. "I need to get a few things out of the back before you park it."

"Yes, ma'am." He motioned towards a group dressed as he was, in red jackets and black trousers. "Come help Mrs. Beaumont with her things."

Mary Claire felt foolish. She was wandering around like a damn tourist, still carrying her dress and overnight bag. She owned the place, for heaven's sake. But never had she imagined it would turn out to be so magnificent. She couldn't stop herself, going from room to room admiring the detail. Graham must have dropped a pretty penny doing this. He'd even had an elevator installed.

There were people milling about everywhere but no one Mary Claire knew. She needed to get rid of her bag and dress. She went up the stairs and down the hallway, glancing into the rooms she passed along the way.

The door to the room she chose wasn't closed all the way. She pushed it open. Well, Graham hadn't been entirely truthful. He'd said the library was the only room still unfinished. This one was just the way she remembered. No curtains and no furniture other than the pile of mattresses in the center. The mattresses had been covered, made up, she supposed, in case this room too was needed for overnight guests.

A hint of movement and then a disembodied voice from the little alcove on the far side of the room startled her.

"Hello." Graham raised himself from the chair that sat by the window.

Only two syllables and her knees felt like they'd turned to rubber.

"I didn't know you were here already." He said.

Mary Claire struggled to find her voice. "I…I didn't know you were on this continent."

"Anna Bell didn't tell you?"

Mary Claire shook her head.

"Guess she's a lot like her mother." He stepped from the alcove into the room. "Actually, we've become quite good friends. She visits me nearly every time she's in Great Britain."

"Imagine that." Mary Claire's voice sounded strained even to her own ears. She cleared her throat. "Graham, the house, the grounds, it's so beautiful. I had no idea it would be so, so grand."

He nodded. "Hank said you hadn't been out here since the renovations were completed."

"No, I, I just couldn't…" She didn't finish the sentence.

"You look well."

Her "thank you," was followed by an awkward silence, then, "How have you been?"

He raised his eyebrows, then shrugged, but didn't speak.

His hair was going gray at the temples which only made him look sexier. That, combined with the sun bronzed hue of his face and arms, for some reason, made her angry. Irrational, she knew, but how dare he look so damn good! And he could tell her only that she looked, *well?*

He walked over and stood beside her, staring down at her.

What was he doing? Coming closer to get a better view of her wrinkles? Her posture stiffened.

"Mary Claire, I would have loved living here with you, raising our child. But we weren't given that. I know it's too late for children but I'd still…"

"Graham, don't." She didn't let him finish. She looked up at him ready to utter some more platitudes about leaving the past in the past and that they were old enough to know better and going on with their lives. She didn't get the chance. She would have sworn she saw sparks shoot from his eyes as he reached out and slammed the door closed.

"Don't what, Mary Claire!" He spat the words. "Don't disturb your nice placid life? Don't make you feel anything? Don't tell you that I still love you? That I've had sex with at least five different women in the past six years and all of them added together couldn't equal what happened between you and me right there?" He pointed to the stack of mattresses. "That I've loved you every goddamn day of my life since I saw you pounding on that piece of stone in the middle of the night thirty years ago in Louisville? Don't what?"

He'd ruined it. Ruined her calm, calculated response. She looked at his face, at the raw emotion that blazed at her from those green eyes and felt her own defenses start to give way. Crumble, bit by bit until she stood helpless in front of him.

Things never went the way she planned when she was near him. She let her dress and the overnight bag drop to the floor and held her arms out toward him.

"Don't ever leave me again," she whispered.

Chapter Sixteen

Mary Claire wished that infernal bird would shut-up. By the time she realized it wasn't a bird but her cell phone that was producing the annoying chirp, it had stopped. The sound of an old-fashioned telephone ring next permeated the air waves, followed by a raspy male voice.

"Hey. I'm sorry. Guess I'm still fighting jet lag. I fell asleep. I'll be down in a few minutes." Graham clicked the phone off.

"Oh God, what time is it?" Mary Claire groaned as her phone started chirping again.

"According to Anna Bell, about ten minutes until picture time."

Mary Claire had located her phone. "Hello."

Anna Bell's voice came through so loud that even Graham could hear her.

"Mother, where in the world are you? I've had an army looking for you. Jimmy said you got here hours ago."

"I did. I've… I've just been looking around. I'm getting dressed now."

"Liar." Graham mouthed the word as he held his hand toward Mary Claire to help her from the make-shift bed.

"Mother, I really need to talk to you before you come down, which room are you in?"

"Why, Anna Bell?"

"I just need to go over the particulars of the ceremony with you."

"We can talk about it when I come down."

"But there's something you need to know. Something I should have…"

Graham took Mary Claire's phone from her hand and spoke into it. "She already does, darling. We'll be down shortly." He clicked the off button on the phone and dropped it onto the mattress. He wrapped his arms around Mary Claire's naked body and kissed her soundly before he took her hand and led her to the shower in the adjoining bathroom.

****

Anna Bell was a beautiful bride. Mary Claire watched as they walked toward the improvised altar in front of the astrolabe sculpture. The sculpture was also decked with hydrangeas. She wished John could be here to see her, to see Anna Bell.

Just then Sissy reached over and took Mary Claire's hand and squeezed it, like she knew what Mary Claire had been thinking. Mary Claire gave Sissy a quick glance, then looked on down the row at Caroline and Clay before she turned her attention back to her daughter and her daughter's father.

Dinner was over, they'd cut the cake, proposed the toasts, and most everyone was finished with dessert. The sun had set and the dancing was ready to begin. Mary Claire sat on the low stone wall that separated the open terrace from the swimming pool. Everyone seemed to be having a good time, even her father. She watched as Clay, surrounded by a crowd of men, delivered the punch line to one of his famous jokes. Ben came over and sat beside her.

"Hiding out?"

"No. Just taking a breather. Observing."

"I know Anna Bell is the star of the show today," he turned to look at his baby sister, "but you look positively radiant."

She gave him a wry smile. "Is that so?"

He nodded, then leaned over closer to her. "Heard you went AWOL before this shebang started. You wasn't off having a highland fling, was you?"

"Ben!" She punched him in the arm.

He laughed and patted her on the leg. "He's okay, Mary Claire. I talked to him a while. Interesting fellow." He got up and walked toward the crowd.

Ben had come to the wedding by himself. He'd finally given up choosing dates from the twenty-five to thirty-year-old age group. Mary Claire watched him as he sat down by Judy Reynolds. Judy was divorced, a grandmother, still very attractive, and in Mary Claire's opinion, a nice person. She hoped something developed between them. Besides, Judy was a Baptist. Lord, Mary Claire thought, Mother would be so happy to finally have one of her children hooked up with a Baptist.

The band started playing. "Cel-e-brate good times, come on." blared from the speakers.

Mary Claire got up and followed the path Ben had taken back to the party. She paused and chatted along the way when a few people stopped her to offer congratulations or comments. She was almost back to the table where she'd left her drink when the band leader's voice echoed across the space. "It's time for the traditional father-daughter dance. We're going to start off with the bride and her father."

"Oh, no." Mary Claire changed direction, hurrying toward the band when a hand grabbed her arm. It was Sissy.

"Oh, Sissy, just a minute." Mary Claire tried to extract her arm from Sissy's grasp. "I need to get up there to tell them…"

Sissy held on tighter. "No you don't."

"But Sissy, everyone's already talking because he walked her down the aisle."

"Then let them. Come here and sit down."

Mary Claire sat in front of the drink she'd abandoned earlier. She picked it up and downed it.

"Anna Bell and I discussed this at length before she decided to do it."

"But Sissy, it'll be an awful scandal."

"Oh Mary Claire, don't you think it's time to clean the skeletons out of the closet?"

Anna Bell and Graham were on the dance floor. The music had started.

"Oh God, I need another drink."

"You can't keep worrying forever about who knows what. It'll suck the life right out of you and keep you from ever building a life with him. They'll talk for a while, but let them. They'll forget soon enough. By the time Christmas rolls around, all they'll remember will be how well you fed them and how free the alcohol flowed. They'll all be clamoring for invitations to your parties."

"Oh dear, I think my mother is about to have a stroke." Mary Claire pointed toward Caroline.

Sissy chuckled.

There was a brief lull in the music, and the band leader's voice rang out. "The rest of the fathers and daughters, please join us on the dance floor."

Maybe she'd already had one drink too many, Mary Claire thought when she looked up and saw Clay coming toward her. Was her father really going to ask her to dance?

She smiled at him when he walked up to the table.

"I'm taking your mother home. She's not feeling well."

Mary Claire tried to hide her disappointment. "Oh, okay. Did you say goodbye to Anna Bell?"

"She's busy." He stared toward the dance floor where Anna Bell and Graham were still dancing. "Goodnight." He turned and left.

"Goodnight, Daddy." Mary Claire propped her elbows on the table and covered her face with her hands. She was still sitting like that two minutes later.

"May I have this dance?"

Mary Claire kept her elbows on the table but moved so that her chin now rested in her hands. She looked up at Graham, at the incredibly handsome face that she noticed also had crinkles around the eyes. She started laughing.

"Oh, what the hell. Why not."

He took her hand and led her onto the dance floor. He wrapped his arms around her and they danced. It didn't matter if the music was slow or fast, they danced at the same speed until the band stopped playing.

Chapter Seventeen

September

Mary Claire sat in the library at Castleton Downs and stared at the walnut paneled wall. It simply didn't belong. She had measured and re-measured and according to the length of the hallway and the dining room next to the library, there was four feet of missing space somewhere.

The contractor was working upstairs reconfiguring the three rooms at the end of the south hallway into a new master suite. When he was finished with that, he would begin on the library, if she could ever figure out what she wanted done.

Much to her mother's chagrin, Mary Claire had given up even the pretense of trying to behave properly. Oh, her official residence was still the house she had shared with John, but she spent most nights with Graham in the penthouse apartment. And as soon as the work upstairs and in the library was finished, they would move into Castleton Downs. Neither of them had mentioned getting married, and for now, it didn't matter. At least not to Mary Claire. She was happy.

She went upstairs and borrowed a hammer and a pry bar from one of the workmen and then headed back to the library. She was sure the missing four feet of space was behind the walnut paneling. It was probably covering nothing more than water pipes and heating ducts from the turn of the twentieth century, but it had to go. She thought about asking the workmen upstairs to remove the wall, but she'd seen them in demolition mode. Even if she had determined that it needed to come down, the material had to be saved. Those walnut panels were beautiful and could be reused or sold for another restoration project.

She used the same painstaking attention to detail in her deconstruction of the wall as she did in the construction of her sculptures. When she finally had the first panel ready to move aside, she stepped back, swiped the dust from her face and took a deep breath. She moved the panel then picked up a flashlight and shone it into the opening. She gasped, laid the flashlight aside and started on the next panel with renewed fervor.

That's how Graham found her six hours later, with three-quarters of the paneling gone and still carefully removing nails from the next one.

"What the hell?" His voice held a note of disbelief.

She whirled around and greeted him with a look of utter triumph.

"What is all that?"

"I don't know. I haven't looked at any of it yet. I just wanted to get it all uncovered."

"Why didn't you have the contractor's men do this?"

"It's my discovery. I wanted to enjoy it. Besides they went home two hours ago. And what if it's something we don't want anyone to see?"

"Well, am I allowed to look?"

"Sure. I'm ready to quit anyway." She laid her tools aside and walked over to stand beside him.

Graham was shaking his head. "Why would someone do this?"

"I don't know." She brushed the dirt off her hands.

The walnut paneling had concealed a wall of shelves, built around a Chippendale hi-boy secretary, and filled with books.

"It's like finding a buried treasure." Mary Claire giggled.

Graham took one of the books from its resting place, blew the dust off, and opened it. Other than it's age, there was nothing special about it. It looked like a normal book. He pulled another one off the shelf. Same thing. And still another. "That's the damnedest thing I've ever seen."

"I think it's exciting. Even if they are just plain old books. I plan on examining every single one of them." Mary Claire reached for his hand. "Starting tomorrow. Would you care to join me in nice relaxing bath?"

"I'd love to join you, but I'm not sure how relaxing it'll turn out to be."

"The contractor said the idea of the built-in glass block tub with the surrounding overflow drain was a great idea for the new master suite."

"He did?"

"Yes. Said it would save the floor and the ceiling beneath it from water damage from running over the tub like someone has done several times with the claw-foot one."

"I haven't run it over, have you?"

"No. but I thought it was better to let him think that than tell him it was just us splashing it all out, while you went spear fishing for the mermaid!"

He leaned his head back and laughed. "Spear fishing for the mermaid?"

"Uh-huh."

He followed her up the stairs.

****

Graham and Mary Claire were cuddled on the sofa in the study of the apartment. The television was on, tuned to the local eleven o'clock news. Graham was trying to read the financial section of a London newspaper.

"Who was Andrew McCullough?" Mary Claire asked through a yawn.

Graham didn't answer.

"Earth to McCullough. Earth to McCullough!" Mary Claire pinched his arm.

He laid the paper aside. "What? I'm trying to earn a living here."

She rolled her eyes. "Who was Andrew McCullough?"

He wrapped his arms around her. "I give up. Who?"

"Oh, quit being so aggravating."

"Seriously, I really don't have the foggiest. Where'd you come up with that name?"

"The books behind the wall. That's who they all belonged to. It's a collection of works on animal husbandry and equine veterinary science. He even wrote some of them."

"Oh, wait a minute. He was the one who…" Graham stopped abruptly.

"The one who what?" Mary Claire twisted her head around to look at him.

"Never mind. It's not important."

She moved his arms from her and sat up straight, then faced him. "What is it, Graham?"

She wasn't going to let it go. He sighed and then took his glasses off, scrunched up his face and, pinched the bridge of his nose. "He was killed."

"So…why didn't you just say that?"

Graham looked into her eyes and grasped both her arms. He pulled her to him so that her face was resting on his chest. Her ear was just below his mouth. "He was killed by a horse. Kicked and stomped to death."

"Oh." The word was a chirp, barely audible.

They'd still never talked about it, about the accident that had claimed the life of their child. Neither of them had mentioned it.

She raised her face to meet his gaze. She blinked rapidly as tears spilled down her cheeks. "I'm so sorry, Graham."

He held on to her tighter. "For what?"

"For being so stupid. For stepping behind that horse. I knew better. I didn't even think about what I was doing." She swallowed hard. "Can you ever forgive me?"

"God, Mary Claire, I'm the one who should be asking forgiveness. I should never have let you near that horse. It was my job to move him. It wasn't your fault. If anyone is to blame, it's me."

She was shaking her head. "No, Graham. I'm the one…"

He put his fingers to her lips. "Don't. I never blamed you, not once. I was distant because of my own guilt. I was sure you blamed me."

"I didn't. I thought you were blaming me."

Mary Claire was rocking side to side. He tightened his hold as the pent up grief flowed from her. He leaned his head back trying to staunch the flow of his own tears. He held her and felt his heart shatter into a million pieces with each sob that tore from her body.

"I love you, Mary Claire, my Annabel Lee. I love you more than my life."

He shifted to situate her more comfortably. He grabbed the remote from the floor and clicked off the television. He reached up with his left arm and pulled a chenille throw from the back of the sofa and spread it over them.

Her tears splashed on his hand. Cathartic, healing, like the waters of baptism, renewing his heart and cleansing his soul with each drop that fell.

Chapter Eighteen

Mary Claire put a fork full of Ida's homemade spinach salad into her mouth. Sissy and Ida had come for a visit and brought lunch with them.

Graham was away for three weeks tending to business matters in London and Edinburgh. So instead of driving to and from town everyday, Mary Claire was staying at Castleton Downs.

"What in the world even made you think to look behind the paneling?" Sissy asked.

The three women were sitting around a folding card table in the library enjoying their repast.

Mary Claire swallowed a sip of iced tea. "Because the measurements were off. All the other formal rooms in the house are perfectly symmetrical. This one wasn't. Plus, the different woods.

"Different woods?"

"Everything in here, with the exception of that wall, was made of chestnut."

"That big old secretary looks like the one that used to be in the front room at Beaumont House," Ida said.

"It does." Sissy agreed as she stared at the piece. "I hated that monstrosity. It belonged to Jackson's momma's family. I got rid of it soon after she died. I always preferred the look of the French antiques." She took a sip of her iced tea. "Did you find anything in the secret drawer?"

"The what?" Mary Claire asked.

"The secret drawer. Those old things all have a secret compartment built into them."

"Oh, I don't think this one does."

Sissy rose from her chair. "Sure it does." She moved to stand in front of the secretary and studied it for a moment. She removed the center drawer just above the writing surface, stuck her hand back into the opening moving it back and forth, feeling the inner workings of the piece. Then she removed the drawer just above the first drawer. She worked for a moment more then pulled her hand out of the opening holding what looked to be a covered box.

Mary Claire and Ida were both up and standing beside her.

"Oh my gosh, Sissy! How did you do that?" Mary Claire reached out and touched the smooth surface of the wood.

"You just have to know where to look." Sissy handed the box to Mary Claire. "I think there's something in it."

Mary Claire tilted the box to the right and then to the left. She felt the contents slide from side to side. She sat the box on the desk and slid the wooden top from it's grooved track. Inside was a stack of papers tied with a ribbon. Mary Claire carefully untied the bundle and lifted the top page. She unfolded the paper. It appeared to be a handwritten letter. It took her a few seconds to make out the words of the flowing, flowery script.

"Oh dear!" Mary Claire's eyes scanned further down the page.

"What is it?" Sissy asked.

Mary Claire handed the letter to Sissy.

"Well, this will certainly answer some questions." Sissy handed the page on to Ida and then stepped back toward the center of the room to examine the tableau. "I wonder if the contents of that drawer was the reason the wall was blocked up? To make sure no one found the documents?"

"But why not just get rid of all of it? The whole kit and caboodle?" Mary Claire posed the question. "Why not just burn the books and the piece of furniture too if they wanted to get rid of it?"

Sissy shook her head. "I don't know. But at least we now know why the Rutherfords and the McCulloughs have been at odds for so many years."

****

Mary Claire spent the afternoon examining the rest of the papers. Talk about a scandal. The letters were correspondence between Amelia Castleton, Mary Claire's great-great grandmother, and her cousin, Chester Kidwell, Esq., Attorney at Law. Other papers were sworn affidavits and handwritten copies of what looked to be gambling debts and statements of indebtedness for gentlemen's clubs and common taverns.

Grandma Castleton was trying to figure out if she had any legal recourse against her son-in-law, one Ambrose Rutherford, for the libelous accusations he was making toward her other son-in-law, Alistair McCullough.

Mary Claire picked up the letter from the attorney, the one she'd read first earlier that afternoon and began reading it again.

March 12, 1882

Dear Cousin Amelia,
    Enclosed are the whole of the materials I have obtained on your behalf. Some are quite telling. I understand the delicate nature

of the problem, what with your grandson, young McCullough, due to arrive shortly to begin his studies, and the concern you hold for the well-being of your daughter and your Rutherford grandchildren being of the highest order.

I think it best to confront Rutherford directly with the evidence, being sure to inform him that my office also holds record of the documents, as well as having placed documentation of them in a third location that I deem to be quite secure.

Your concern for the reputation of McCullough, while well founded, should not prove problematic. Rutherford's pronouncements against him will likely not find their way across the Atlantic to cause him trouble. And in the event that some are carried there, McCullough is well enough established so that those who know will pay the accusations no heed.

Along with all that I have included herewith, there is also another matter, of such an indelicate nature, that I hesitate to relate it, but should Rutherford not back down when confronted with the more mundane of the proofs against him, it may become necessary to use this also.

It has to do with a matter that occurred before he brought his family from London to reside with you in Kentucky. It concerns the issue of a child from his consorting with a woman who, although of high birth, had fallen from her family's grace some years before and was no longer received by any of them. The child was possessed of a weak constitution from the start and did not survive long past the third anniversary of its birth. But that it did exist and that it was in fact Rutherford's offspring is well documented.

I shall send my associate, Mr. Bingham Stultz, to call on you and arrange a time for him to be present with you when you present these findings to Rutherford.

If I may be of further assistance, pray do not hesitate to call upon me.

In affection, your cousin,

Chester B. Kidwell, Esquire

Mary Claire then re-read the last letter in the stack.

April 24, 1882

My dear cousin Chester,

It is with a heavy heart that I write to inform you of the death of my son-in-law, Ambrose Rutherford. My daughter discovered her husband's lifeless body hanging from a noose of his own making only yesterday. The interment service will take place tomorrow, here on the grounds of Castleton Downs.

I sought only to have him cease his untruthful utterances against my other daughter's husband and to stop the hemorrhage of money from my grandchildren's legacy. I did not foresee the possibility of his taking his own life when confronted with the leavings of his debaucherous lifestyle.

I shall retain a copy of this correspondence and secure it with the items you sent previously. The entire collection will be maintained in a location known only to me.

In sincerity, I remain,
Your cousin,
Amelia Kidwell Castleton

Mary Claire carried the papers back to the secretary. She stuck her hand into the empty space where the secret drawer had been. She wondered what other secrets were concealed in the antique furniture she walked past every day. The furniture in her own home, in her parents' home, in Sissy's?

She wanted to see how the hidden compartment was constructed. She picked up her flashlight and propped it on the writing surface of the secretary while she twisted and turned every which way trying to see into the void. She finally gave up. Unless she could manage to turn her head one hundred and eighty degrees she wasn't going to be able to see the mechanism.

She sat down on the old sofa that was in the middle of the room and stared at the fireplace directly in front of her. The sofa was one that had been stored in the basement at her house. Anna Bell had particularly liked it , so Mary Claire had saved it, intending to give it to her for her first apartment. Mary Claire smiled. The old sofa hadn't made the trip to California. Anna Bell had never done anything the way Mary Claire expected. The fact that she was sitting here in the unfinished library at Castleton Downs, contemplating spending the rest of her days on this estate with Graham was proof of that.

The air was beginning to chill. It would be nice to cuddle up on the old sofa with a fire crackling in the grate. She got up, retrieved her flashlight, and carried it to the fireplace. She got down on her knees and leaned in, trying to see if the chimney had been relined.

Like the desk earlier, she couldn't see much from this angle. She sat down and scooted into the fire pit so that her back was against the firebrick wall. She pushed the button on the flashlight and pointed it above her. The beam from the light was swallowed by the darkness. Oh well, so much for that idea. She wasn't willing to chance burning the place to the ground.

She was having trouble manipulating her body to get out of the fireplace. She began rocking from side to side, inching her way forward with each movement. When she'd made it to the front edge of the opening, she rolled the flashlight across the floor into the room and grabbed hold of the outside edge of the opening to help pull herself out. When she pulled backwards, she felt one of the bricks move.

The mortar must be loose. This chimney for sure hadn't been restored yet. She pulled herself the rest of the way out and then rose up on her knees and turned to examine the loose brick. Funny, the mortar looked fine. She wiggled the brick. Definitely loose. She tried the one above it. It was stuck tight. She returned her attention to the loose one and this time gave it a slight tug. She felt it slide toward her. She pulled again and the brick came sliding out.

"Wow! This whole room is like a great big treasure vault." A surge of excitement shot through her. She crawled over and grabbed the flashlight and then shone it into the opening and felt her elation dissipate. There was nothing inside except a metal lever. Probably controlled the damper. She pulled on one of her work gloves, then reached in and pressed the lever.

A sliding noise. But it was behind her, not inside the chimney. "Hum, not the damper." She reached into the hole again and this time, pulled the lever. Again, she heard the sliding noise. It took four times of pushing and pulling the lever before she figured out where the sliding noise was coming from.

The kick plate panel closest to the fireplace under the left side window seat was opening and closing with each adjustment of the lever. Mary Claire lay flat out on her stomach and shined the flashlight into the space. There was something in it.

She wasn't crazy about the idea of sticking her hand into still yet one more dark spidery space. She grabbed the borrowed pry bar that was still lying on the bench of the window seat and used it to pull the contents of the secret compartment out into the open.

She knocked the dust and spider webs off two string tied folders. One was filled with newspaper pages. The other held three leather bound journals.

She slipped the first of the journals out the folder. She opened it and began to read.

Chapter Nineteen

Mary Claire didn't mention her new treasures to Graham when he came back. Something was bothering him. He didn't say so, but the fact that he insisted they stay holed up in the apartment since he'd returned was a dead give-away.

The first day he'd made mad passionate love to her in a way that was as impersonal as if he'd been paying for it, and then retreated into an insular shell of silence for hours. He had hardly slept. Two nights in a row, she had awakened to find his side of the bed empty. She'd found him downstairs in his office, buried in paperwork to the extent that he hadn't even looked up when she opened the door.

By the third day, she'd had enough.

He had disappeared down to his office again. This time when he didn't look up at the sound of the door opening, she didn't close it softly and retreat, the way she'd done the previous two nights. She stepped into the room and slammed the door with all the might she could muster.

"Bloody hell!" He jumped and knocked a stack of papers to the floor. "Are you trying to give me a heart attack?"

"No. I'm just trying to get your attention."

"Well, I'd say you accomplished that." He leaned back in his chair and took his glasses off. He squeezed the bridge of his nose and closed his eyes.

She crossed the room, stopping to pick up the fallen papers and replace them on his desk, then moved behind him, massaging his temples with the tips of her fingers.

"What's wrong, Graham? You're scaring me."

He reached up and took her hand and pulled her around the chair and down onto his lap.

"Nothing is wrong. Not one thing."

"Then why have you been acting this way?"

"What way?"

"So shut off and distant."

"Distant?" He raised his eyebrows. "I thought we'd been in quite close contact several times since I've been back."

"You know what I mean." Her expression was serious.

"You're right. I do." He was trailing his fingers down the bare flesh of her arm. "I'm sorry, but I wanted to make sure I had it all worked out just right before I presented it to you."

"What?"

"I'm quitting."

"Quitting?"

He nodded.

"Quitting what?"

"Work." He smiled. "God, it feels good to say that. It's the first time I've actually said it out loud. I'm retiring. I'm going to turn it all over to Jamie. All except the horses. We're going to split that off as a separate corporation that Hamish and I will control."

"That's it?" Mary Claire let herself relax.

"Well, not all of it, exactly."

Her body tensed again.

"Do you like the apartment upstairs?"

"Yes."

"Do you like your house better?"

She considered her answer. "Not better, just for different reasons. What else do you have up your sleeve?"

"What if we don't end up living at Castleton Downs?"

"But, I thought that was your dream."

"I think it may suite someone else's dream better. How would you feel about giving it to Anna Bell and Brian?"

"But what about Sean? I thought the reason you bought it in the first place was for him?"

"It was, but if you'll remember, I don't own it any longer."

She waved a hand in the air like that little detail was of no consequence.

"Besides, things have changed."

"Graham, I'm tired of playing twenty questions. Just spill it."

"Sean has enrolled in seminary, the Josephinum, in Columbus, Ohio. He wants to be a priest."

Mary Claire's mouth dropped open. "You're kidding."

"No, He's been wrestling with it for years. It really didn't come as a surprise."

"What kind of an assignment would a priest who can build bridges end up with?"

"I don't know. Maybe as a missionary in a third world country that needs help building infrastructure?"

"Oh, I didn't think of that. Wow." She scrutinized his face. "Are you okay with it? With him becoming a priest?"

"Yes. Like I said, it didn't surprise me. He's always taken his faith seriously."

They sat quietly for a few moments before Mary Claire asked. "What makes you think Anna Bell and Brian would leave California?"

"Because their dream is to open a winery with a bed and breakfast and a restaurant, al la Sonoma, right here in the Bluegrass State."

"How do you know that?"

"Because, my dear, unlike some people, I've learned to talk to my children. All three of them."

She wrapped her arms around his neck and leaned her face toward his until their lips met. She twined her fingers through the hair at the nape of his neck and pressed her lips harder against his as her tongue probed his open mouth.

He nudged her off his lap onto her feet and then stood himself.

"Shall we repair to the bedchamber, m' lady?"

"Of course, m' lord."

****

Mary Claire waited until they finished dinner the next evening before she showed the letters, newspaper articles, and journals to Graham.

"Where did all this come from?" He sorted through the first stack of papers they'd found.

"The library at Castleton Downs. Sissy found that bundle hidden in a secret drawer in that big old secretary."

"Really?"

"Yes. The rest, I found in a hollow space under the window seat, left of the fireplace."

"So, what's it all say?" He was now turning the pages of one of the journals.

"I think you should read it for yourself."

"Why?"

"So you can help me decide if I should give it to my father."

"Okay, you've lost me."

"That part," she pointed to the bundle of letters and papers, "was written by our common ancestor, great-great Grandma Castleton." Mary Claire sat down beside him. "It tells the real story about what happened. Why the families got mad at each other in the first place. The rest is written by her daughter, the Rutherford one. It explains the perpetuation of the feud."

He opened the journal again and looked at the first page. "Mary Claire, I hate reading this flowery script."

"Bite the bullet on this one, McCullough." She was smiling when he looked at her. "For the future of the alliance. Now, I'm going to go take a bath." She pointed toward the journal. "And there will be a test later. No Cheating."

He reached for his reading glasses on the side table.

Graham started with the bundle from the secretary. According to Grandmother Castleton, her son-in-law, Ambrose Rutherford, was a man of weak moral fiber. More prone to strong drink and wagering than overseeing his share of Castleton Industries, he found himself with massive gambling losses. When on the verge of losing everything, including his own family's estate, his wife's brother-in-law, Alistair McCullough, paid Rutherford twice the worth for his shares in Castleton Industries.

Out from under the weight of his crushing debt and feeling flush with the monies McCullough had paid him, he embarked on another gambling spree which did result in the loss of his family's home.

He then moved his wife and children to America, to live with his wife's mother at Castleton Downs, the home she had built some years before in her native Kentucky.

The new surroundings did nothing to improve Rutherford's behavior. When pressed to explain his presence in America, he maligned McCullough, saying the Scot had cheated him of his interest in Castleton Industries.

When his mother-in-law heard of his actions, she threatened him with expulsion from her home and public exposure if he didn't stop.

Graham replaced the letters and documents into the folder Mary Claire had given him. A shiver went through his body. He felt a strong connection with Grandmother Castleton. He'd always know the old gal had been a shrewd business woman. He'd gone through the archives, read every single page of records, when he'd taken over as head of Castleton-McCullough. Amelia Castleton too had eventually sold her share of the company to Alistair McCullough. That was where Graham's knowledge of her had ended.

From the contents of the folder, it looked like she had conducted every aspect of her life in the same way she did her business life. She made sure all her ducks were in a row before she acted.

He opened the first of the journals and began to read. It was hard to read, not because of the flowery script, but because of the content.

Mary Margaret Rutherford had committed to paper what she could not speak, could not share with anyone. The books contained a woman's lament, a daughter's regret, and a mother's horror.

London, June 20, 1866

Ambrose is not home again. It is past the mid of night and into Sunday. If he does not stumble in soon, I pray he will pass the rest of the night in his study. I do not know how I shall endure if again I am forced to lie beside him smelling the scent of another woman and his own disgusting smell of passion on his person.

How many times these past months have I wished I had listened to my mother. But it is too late now. The old platitude of beauty being only skin deep is appropriate when speaking of Ambrose. He is endowed with the eyes of an angel and the soul of Lucifer. But then Lucifer was an angel too, was he not?

Dear God, the child within me rebels this moment even I think ill of Ambrose. Such a mighty kick against my ribs. It is a Rutherford for certain, most probably a boy, all say, for the way it is situated so low. But maybe he kicks from hunger. I am barely able to crawl from the bed I am so weak of it.

But it is the only way I may insure the child stays small, so when he comes all will believe the birth is early. I pray I do not kill him in my effort to save myself from shame.

Once he started, Graham couldn't tear himself away. Mary Margaret Rutherford wrote with such passion, such angst. And the words explained so much.

Lexington, August 12, 1888

I am in hell. My prayers fall to the ground instead of rising to God in Heaven. I have prayed to God, to Jesus, to Mary the Mother of God, and even burned incense as the Catholics do, hoping my prayers may rise on the smoke, but they go nowhere.

My son cannot be blamed for his paternity, for the inheritance of his father's nature. I, and only I, am to blame for what has taken place. If I could have admitted my own culpability and acknowledged that I indeed knew what caused Ambrose to take his own life, perhaps William would have turned his life from this hatred he has taken on. This fear that my sister's son, Andrew

McCullough, would snatch away Castleton Downs from him as he always believed my sister's husband had stolen Castleton Industries from Ambrose.

How do I live knowing that William has purposefully caused the death of his cousin? Would that I had not strolled into the barn in the afternoon of last to sit quietly and listen to the sound of the horses. That I had not heard William coo and croon to the horse that killed Andrew. And then laugh as he fed the creature apples and carrots in reward for a job well done. A job he had been trained to do, rear and stomp at the smell of a particular odor.

I sat in the room as William welcomed Andrew back to Castleton Downs with the gift of a handkerchief steeped in the scent of wood balm. I listened as William lured him to the barn in what I now know was the pretense of tending to an injured horse.

The hardest is watching my son and knowing that he feels no remorse in his action. What kind of monster have I let loose from my body? Is it because he was conceived in a sinful, lustful act outside of wedlock? Because I damaged him as he formed, in my self-imposed starvation?

My mother is not well, and I fear she will soon be gone from us too. If I were possessed of more fortitude, I would put an end to William and then to myself. But I cannot, for I fear the fires of an eternal hell more than the hell of this earthly existence.

I will stay here to continue my prayers and beg forgiveness and to watch William so that he can do no more harm.

Graham turned the page to the last entry.

March 18, 1893

I have won a small victory. William is to be married three months hence, and has undertaken a redecorating project he says is at the request of his intended bride. It is merely a ruse to destroy Andrew's work. I adamantly insisted the work remain where it sits, so instead of destroying it, William will have it covered.

At this very moment, the carpenters are erecting a wall in the library to completely obliterate the collection of important works Andrew assembled and those he wrote. William also instructed that Mother's old secretary desk be covered. I suppose in the case that any legal documents be stored there, noting bequests to other of his McCullough cousins.

Mother is confined to her bed these past months and is long past any recognition of those she has known her entire life. Having also learned that Mother's cousin and solicitor, Mr. Kidwell, died some months back, has strengthened William's assuredness that Castleton Downs is his to do with as he pleases.

I fear my future daughter-in-law comes to the match with reluctance. She is warm toward me, but quite reserved when dealing with William. Her family's fortunes have suffered a reversal in recent years and I have heard that she received a good deal of pressure from her mother in accepting William's proposal.

At least, from what I have observed, William is not inclined to make the conquest of any lady that catches his fancy, as was his father. William pours his energies into his business ventures. I pray all goes smoothly with the marriage.

Graham closed the book and laid it on top of the other two. He picked up the remaining folder and looked at the newspapers it held. One contained the account of Andrew McCullough's death. Most of them had stories relating to William Rutherford's businesses. One contained the death notice of Amelia Kidwell Castleton. And then one held the emblazoned headline:

LEXINGTON BUSINESSMAN, RUTHERFORD, LOST IN SINKING OF THE TITANIC

The last paper from June 13, 1915, was folded open to the society page.

Mrs. Mary Rose Rutherford (nee Carlisle), widow of the late William Rutherford, held the hand of her four-year-old son, Cassius Marcellus Rutherford, in the garden of her parent's beautifully restored antebellum home and spoke her wedding vows to Mr. Theodore J. Crouse, while her elder son, Benjamin Pierce Rutherford, looked on. Mr. Crouse of Lexington, will shortly remove his new family to Washington City where he will assume his duties as the newly appointed Under Secretary to the Head of the War Department.

Graham laid the paper aside and glanced at the clock. It was just past four in the morning. He took off his glasses, leaned his head back and promptly fell asleep.

****

Graham turned out to be no help at all to Mary Claire in deciding whether to turn over the new found information to her father. "It's up to you," he'd said.

She finally called Hank and asked him to meet her at Castleton Downs the next morning for breakfast.

"Didn't know you could still cook," he said when she set a plate of crisp bacon on the table.

"You'd be surprised what I can still do." Mary Claire turned back to the stove to take a pan of biscuits out of the oven. "Though, I'm not sure this qualifies as cooking. Sticking a pan of Ida's biscuits in the oven and crisping up some pre-cooked bacon doesn't take a lot of talent."

Hank laughed and slathered one of the steaming biscuits with butter. "So what is it you want me to look at?"

Mary Claire gave him a summary of the articles she'd found. After they ate, she took him to the library to show him the hiding place and then pointed him to the secretary where she'd laid out the documents.

"Wow." Hank closed the third journal and laid it down. "I think you have to show it to him. And not just because of Graham. You may not even remember, you were really little. The year Mom's Aunt Julia and Uncle Fred came from Baltimore to spend Christmas with us. They gave Dad an antique book they'd found in London. It was a compendium on the breeding and care of horses for racing. I remember he threw a god awful fit over it. Burned it in the fireplace as soon as they left. It was written by Andrew McCullough."

"No, I don't remember it."

"My point is—that kind of blind hate, just because of a name, well, it's wrong. Plain and simple. He needs to know the whole feud was based on a lie."

"Okay." Mary Claire frowned as she gathered the material up and placed it in a leather satchel. "You don't think he'd burn this too, do you?"

Hank draped an arm across her shoulder and pulled her against him in a gesture of brotherly affection. "Wouldn't put it past him."

****

Since Anna Bell was staying in California for the holiday and Mary Claire had agreed to spend Thanksgiving in Scotland with Graham's family, Caroline insisted on having a family dinner the Sunday before Thanksgiving.

Ben called Mary Claire and thanked her for having the guts to ruin Caroline's Thanksgiving plans because he was now free to spend the holiday at Judy's. They had started dating right after Anna Bell and Brian's wedding. Ben had confided to Mary Claire he planned on asking Judy to marry him soon. Knowing Ben that could either mean before Christmas or sometime before the end of the decade.

Mary Claire carried the satchel containing the letters, newspapers and journals. She held it toward Clay as she and Graham were leaving after the dinner on Sunday.

"Daddy, we found these things hidden in the library at Castleton Downs. I'd like you to read all of them and then give them back to me."

"What the hell is it?" He took the bag from her.

"Letters and diaries written by Amelia Castleton and Mary Margaret Rutherford."

He made a face. "Mary Claire, I ain't got the time to…"

"You have to." She interrupted him and took his free hand with both of hers. Her eyes were pleading. "Please, Daddy, just read it."

"Well, if it's that important, I'll try."

"It is." She said as she went out the door.

Graham nodded to Clay as he followed Mary Claire over the threshold.

Clay called after them. "I ain't promising. Only if I get the time."

Chapter Twenty

December

Mary Claire couldn't believe her plan had come together so perfectly. Considering she hadn't even mentioned it until she and Graham had returned from their Thanksgiving trip to Scotland.

She checked her list again to make sure all the out-of-town guests had accommodations. Everyone was coming to Castleton Downs for Christmas—her family, Graham's family, even John's family.

She'd known getting Clay and Caroline to come was going to be an iffy proposition, seeing as she was on both their lists these days—Clay's for asking him to read the documents from the library and Caroline's because she'd missed Decorating Saturday, for the first time ever. Mary Claire knew there had been plenty of eager hands to help, but Caroline was still miffed at her for not being there. But the enticement of Anna Bell and Brian being present for Christmas had been enough to persuade them to come.

Mary Claire called the same florist who had done Anna Bell's wedding. A decorating army had descended on Castleton Downs once again. The place looked like a fairy tale. The only thing Mary Claire had not had them do was trim the twelve-foot Fraser fir sitting in the music room. Family and overnight guests would take care of that on Christmas Eve.

She'd been nervous when she'd mentioned to Graham that they should invite Barbara too, since both Sean and Jamie and his family were coming. Graham had surprised her by agreeing.

They had met during the Thanksgiving trip to Scotland. Polly had apologized profusely, when she explained she had asked Barbara and her husband to come for dinner before she knew Graham and Mary Claire were planning to be there.

Mary Claire had been prepared to hate Graham's ex-wife, but she liked Barbara immediately. She didn't think they'd ever be bosom buddies, but she knew she could develop a cordial relationship with the woman. Besides, Barbara was remarried and it was clear she had no designs on Graham.

Irrationally, the one thing Mary Claire did hold against the woman was that she had been the one to see Graham being a daddy. Mary Claire remembered watching as he bounced Jamie's two-year-old son on his knee and rolled in the floor with the little boy's four-year-old sister. Mary Claire needed to insist that he visit his grandchildren more often.

Ida had offered to oversee the food preparation. Mary Claire gladly accepted and had given her the phone number of the the caterer who did Anna Bell's wedding.

The Fed Ex truck pulled away as Mary Claire closed the front door of Castleton Downs and then turned to look at Graham.

"I don't know what I'm going to do with all this and we still have three days to go. We're going to have a house full of gifts and no room for the people."

There was not one square inch of empty space left in the music room or the front parlor. The packages had started arriving the previous week. Yesterday had been a constant stream of delivery vehicles. Mary Claire hadn't considered everyone would ship their packages here to be opened on Christmas morning.

Graham's face lit up. "I've got an idea."

"What?"

"Mary Queen of Scots' new barn."

Mary Claire scrunched up her face and shook her head. "What?"

"The barn I had built. It's for a horse I haven't told you about yet. A filly named Mary Queen of Scots. She's still in Scotland, but the barn is finished. It's brand new, clean and heated. We could put up a tree and take all the gifts out there. It might be a little inconvenient to have to cart everyone down there, but it could work."

"That's a wonderful idea. We could set up a few tables have some hors 'd oeuvres and sweets."

"Okay. Jamie, Sean, and I will take care of getting everything set up this afternoon." He looked at his watch. "Speaking of Jamie and Sean, I'd better get going, their flight should be landing in a little over an hour."

"That entire barn is for one horse?" His comment had just registered with Mary Claire.

"All queens have an entourage. This one's no different."

"Did you name her Mary for any particular reason?"

He picked up his keys off the hall table. "Well, we were going to call her Gertrude, Queen of Scots, but it didn't have the same ring to it." He pulled the door open and then stopped. He grabbed Mary Claire around the waist and pulled her to him. He gave her a big kiss. "I really wanted to name her after the lady who rules this Scot, the queen of my heart."

"Oh, puh-lease." She shoved away from him. "Go to the airport." She watched him from the open doorway as he drove away. He'd been on cloud nine ever since he found out his entire family was coming.

Mary Claire waded into the sea of packages in the front parlor and started sorting them. She'd been at it for a while when she heard the ring tone indicating a vehicle was coming up the drive. They had left the gate open because it had proved nearly impossible to get anything done besides run to answer the call box and then buzz the gate open for still another delivery.

She hoped it was Judy and her daughter, Leslie. Judy had volunteered to help Mary Claire today and Leslie was going to be on call as a baby sitter, if needed.

Mary Claire stepped over two boxes and pulled the sheers aside to peek out the window. She didn't recognize the car. She let the curtain fall back into place and made her way across the room. Probably a stray sightseer wandering in since the gate was open. Mary Claire opened the door just as the car pulled up to the front of the house and stopped.

Anna Bell got out of the driver's side and put her arms above her head to stretch. She turned toward the house.

Mary Claire met her half-way up the walk. She embraced Anna Bell and kissed the side of her face. "I'm so happy to see you, but what are you doing here already? And where are Brian and the children?"

"They're in Fort Thomas at Brian's parents'."

Mary Claire stepped back, still holding on to Anna Bell's arms and looked at her daughter's face. "Is everything okay? I mean you two aren't having problems are you?"

"Everything is fine, Mother. Brian and I are good, really good."

Mary Claire put her hand to her chest and sighed.

"I just thought it would be nice if they had some time together without me. I am a part of their family, but I'm not the children's mother. Besides," she looked at Mary Claire and grinned, "I could use a couple of days without the kids. I love them, but I'm not used to being with them twenty-four, seven. Brian said they'll be here early on Christmas Eve."

When the two women entered the house, Anna Bell burst out laughing. "Oh my God! And I thought the decorations for my wedding were over the top."

"Well, I did learn from the best." Mary Claire shut the door behind them.

"Grandmother will love it." Anna Bell turned in a circle and then put her hands on her hips. "On the other hand, Grandmom Caroline will think it's ostentatious and vulgar!"

"Oh, you can be sure of that."

"Is Graham here?"

"No. He went to the airport to pick up Sean and Jamie and Jamie's family."

"Oh." Anna Bell's smile disappeared. "I've never met Jamie." She bit her bottom lip. "Mother, I'm really nervous about this gathering."

"Why?" Mary Claire slid her arm around Anna Bell's waist. "There's no need to be. All of your McCullough family will love you too."

"But what if they shut me out? I've only ever been around Graham by myself or with you all, my family. Not when his family is around."

"It's not a competition, baby. And if you get any cold shoulders or feel isolated, there will be plenty of people here to rescue you. No, this house party is about love. And forgiveness, I hope."

Anna Bell stepped away from Mary Claire's embrace. "What do you mean, forgiveness?"

"Well, Mother and Daddy are coming because you're here and because Ben and Hank and both their families will be here, but I'm still on both their shit lists."

Anna Bell laughed. "Not virgin territory for you."

Mary Claire nodded in agreement. "Sean and Jamie's mother is even coming."

"You're kidding."

"No. I met her when we were in Scotland for Thanksgiving. We got along famously. Her husband is coming too. She remarried about four years ago."

"Well, don't expect me to call Brian's ex and invite her." Anna Bell hesitated. "Are you and Graham going to get married?"

Mary Claire's expression sobered. "I don't know. Probably not."

"Why on earth not?"

"Well he hasn't ask me again, for one thing. And…" Mary Claire sighed. "I know you won't believe this, but I don't think I would marry him even if he did ask, as long as Daddy is alive."

"Mother that is the silliest thing I've ever heard."

"I know, but I think it would be the ultimate insult to him and I just can't do that."

Anna Bell tilted her head back and threw her arms out to her sides. "To quote that venerable sage, Sissy Beaumont, *The things we do for God and family*!"

"Good heavens. I hope my hostessing skills improve. I haven't even let you past the front hall. Let's bring your bags in and you can get freshened up and then come join me in the parlor."

Anna Bell put her hand on Mary Claire's arm. "If it's okay, I thought I'd stay in town at our house. In my old room. Just until Brian and the kids get here."

Mary Claire smiled and nodded. "That's fine, Anna Bell, perfectly fine."

"And Mother, there's one more thing I should tell you before it gets too crazy around here."

"What darling?"

"You're going to be a grandmother."

Tears welled up in Mary Claire's eyes. She wrapped her arms around Anna Bell and hugged her and then alternately ran her hand along the length of Anna Bell's hair and patted her back. "Oh, baby, I'm so happy for you." Mary Claire let go and then stepped back. "We'll have to plan a shopping trip. I'll have to come to California. Do they have baby shops on Rodeo Drive? Oh, we could go to Florida. There are some wonderful places in Palm Beach, on Worth Avenue. Or maybe we could hit New York, or even Paris or London."

"Mother!" Anna Bell interrupted her. "You have been spending entirely too much time with Grandmother. My baby will be perfectly happy with clothes from the Fayette Mall. Just like I was."

Mary Claire laughed and then glanced at Anna Bell's stomach. "Looks like we still have some time to decide on a shopping destination."

"I'm due the middle of July."

Mary Claire slid her arm around Anna Bell's waist and headed them toward the kitchen. "Let's have a celebratory drink. Fruit juice for you and a big glass of iced tea for me. July, huh? Summer babies are good." Mary Claire said as they walked.

Chapter Twenty-One

Jamie walked into the parlor where Anna Bell was sorting the last of the packages. "Why don't you come with us?" He buttoned his jacket as he spoke.

"No. You and Sean probably want to spend some time with…with your dad."

Sean came up behind her. "You're right, we do." He put his arm around her shoulders. "We also want to spend some time with our sister."

Her eyes filled with tears and she leaned over against him.

"You guys ready?" Graham's voice came from the doorway.

"Nearly." Jamie said. "Anna Bell's coming with us."

Anna Bell slipped from Sean's embrace and hurried from the room slowing only as she passed Graham to give him a quick peck on the cheek. "I'll be back in a jiffy." Her voice echoed through the hallway as she sprinted toward the library.

"Mother, do you have an old jacket I can borrow?"

Mary Claire looked up from the table where she and Judy were making place cards. "There are a couple hanging by the door in the utility room next to the kitchen. Why do you need a jacket?"

"I'm going with Graham and the guys to find a tree."

Mary Claire sat back in her chair. "Really?"

"Yes. What about gloves?"

"Top drawer, left hand side, utility room." Mary Claire got up. "Are you sure you should?"

Anna Bell raised her eyebrows. "Mother, I'm not going to play lumberjack. I'm basically taking a walk."

"Of course. Have fun."

Anna Bell turned and ran toward the kitchen.

"I swear she has changed so much since she got married." Mary Claire was still looking toward the doorway where Anna Bell had disappeared.

Judy smiled and kept writing. "You think so?"

"Oh yes. She's like a different person."

"I don't really see it." Judy laid her pen aside and got up to stretch. "You on the other hand, have returned to being Mary Claire Rutherford. The one I used to know. Way back when. The one who picked up and moved to Louisville by herself. The one who goes after what she wants no matter what anyone else thinks." Judy spread her arms out. "I mean, all this finery doesn't change the fact that you and McCullough are shacked up together."

Mary Claire burst out laughing. "Don't I know it. Mother makes it a point to mention that little piece of information every chance she gets."

"Yeah, it really grates on us good Baptists."

Mary Claire stood by the window and watched as Graham, bow saw in hand, and Anna Bell, flanked by Sean and Jamie, walked across the field toward the woods at the far end of the last barn. "Oh, like you and Ben aren't carrying on worse than a couple of rabbits every chance you get." Mary Claire continued to stare out the window.

Judy let out a whoop of laughter as she sat down again and picked up her pen. "Shhh, you'll ruin my reputation. Come on, we're almost done. Let's get these cards finished."

****

Mary Claire was sure she had stepped into the screen of the sappiest, happily-ever-after, clichéd Christmas movie ever. Graham hadn't stopped smiling for three days. The gift opening in the barn had been a great success and now they were ready for the grand finale—the formal dinner.

The doors of the music room had been thrown open to the adjoining hall, creating an ample sized dining area. The hall was set up with buffet stations and the music room with eating tables draped in white cloths trimmed in red, green, and gold. Even the chairs were festooned with swags of live evergreen, intertwined with ribbons, berries, and dried flowers. Ida had outdone herself with the food preparation and presentation. The meal was sumptuous.

Mary Claire didn't think he'd planned it, but as the meal was coming to an end, Graham got up to speak. It took a couple of minutes for the room to quiet down.

"First, I'd like to thank all of you for coming, for making this one of the happiest Christmas celebrations I can recall." He looked directly at Mary Claire's parents. "Clay, Caroline, I'd especially like to thank you for coming." He reached over and squeezed Mary Claire on the shoulder. "And for your daughter."

Caroline's cheeks flushed pink as she gave a nervous smile and then demurely dropped her gaze to rest on her hands folded in her lap. Clay responded with an audible snort.

Unfazed, Graham continued. "Sissy, thank you for coming and bringing your wonderful family. And thank you for your help and friendship."

Sissy smiled and raised her glass to Graham. "You are very welcome, dear boy."

Graham dipped his head to her in acknowledgement. "The coming year will bring a number of changes for me and for my children." He glanced at Jamie, Sean and Anna Bell, each in turn. "I'm stepping down as CEO of Castleton-McCullough and turning the reins over to Jamie."

The sound of surprised whispers filled the room.

"I plan to stay busy here with the horse business and if I can talk Mary Claire into it, some real traveling. Not just flying back and forth to London and Edinburgh. So for those of you who hold a piece of the company in your portfolio, you can be assured your investment is safe and remains in good hands."

Graham left his place at the head of the table and walked over to stand behind Sean. He put his hands on the young man's shoulders. "Sean will be entering seminary next month to begin his study for the priesthood."

The buzz of voices in the room became more audible. Graham waited until they calmed down and then continued. "Barbara and I are extremely proud of him and support his decision completely."

Graham then moved to stand behind Anna Bell. He placed one hand on her shoulder and his other hand on Brian's. "As major as those changes for the boys are, this one is in for the biggest change." He leaned down to kiss her on the cheek. "Anna Bell and Brian will be moving here, to Castleton Downs. They will be opening a bed and breakfast and a restaurant and in a few years hope to have it thriving as a full fledged winery."

Now the room erupted into a roar of chatter. Graham looked at Hank and spoke above the din. "Don't worry Hank. They're not evicting us from the barns. I've already specified the grapes have to go in the fields beyond the woods. The pasture is safe."

"Don't scare me like that." Hank shouted.

The room quieted again when they saw that Graham wasn't finished. "Oh, and one more thing. When you're all congratulating Anna Bell and Brian on the new business, give them a little word of congratulations for the news that they're expecting a baby come July."

That was the end of Graham's speech. Everyone was up, out of their chairs, patting backs, shaking hands, kissing cheeks and smiling. Graham noticed that even Clay couldn't hide the smile that tugged at the corners of his mouth.

****

Mary Claire pulled her jacket tighter around her and leaned her head back to study the sky on this cold January night. She sat on the cast iron bench at the edge of Caroline's rose garden. God, she was tired. It was past midnight but she had to get out of the house, steal some alone time before she went to bed.

Mary Claire had forgotten what it was like to spend so much time with other people. She felt guilty for wanting to escape but coming so close on the heels of their week long Christmas house party at Castleton Downs, these past three weeks at Rutherford Commons was enough to try anyone's sanity.

Her mother had suffered a heart-attack on New Year's Eve and had undergone by-pass surgery on New Year's Day. Mary Claire had moved into Rutherford Commons to help care for Caroline when she was dismissed from the hospital. Caroline was a strong woman, and thankfully, was recovering well ahead of schedule.

This health scare of Caroline's made Mary Claire realize how lucky she was to still have both of her parents. She never really thought of them as old, the way she did Sissy, even though they were only a few years younger. Daddy would be eighty in March. Mary Claire closed her eyes. They'd always just been Mother and Daddy, ever present, ever watchful, ever willing to disapprove.

"Mary Claire?"

She turned to see her father at the end of the garden path, coming toward her. "Hey Daddy. What are you doing out this time of night?"

He stopped next to the bench and took a cigarette and lighter from his jacket pocket. "This is the only time I can enjoy a smoke in peace. After your mother's already asleep."

Mary Claire laughed.

He lit the cigarette and inhaled deeply.

She held her hand out to him. "Give me a puff of that."

He frowned at her but handed her the cigarette.

She took a puff, blew the smoke out, and made a face. "Yuck! How can you stand that?" She handed the cigarette back to him.

"Oh, you'd be surprised what you can make yourself get used to and then be convinced you can't live without it." He took another drag and then dropped the cigarette and crushed it beneath the sole of his boot. "Mary Claire, baby, can you ever forgive me?"

"For what, Daddy?"

"For making your life miserable."

She reached up and grabbed his hand and pulled him down to sit beside her. "What are you talking about?"

"It's not easy to find out your whole life has been based on a lie."

"Are you talking about Anna Bell?"

"No. I'm talking about me." He paused for a moment. "I don't know, maybe I am talking about Anna Bell too. It's all tied up together. All of it because I was taught to hate them cheating, conniving, sons of bitches McCulloughs."

"Daddy, if William Rutherford worked so hard to keep Castleton Downs, how is it that it didn't stay in the family? Why did I never know about it?"

"Best I can recall hearing is that it was sold off right after the old woman, Mary Margaret Rutherford, died. Her grandsons were with their mother and step-father in Washington. My father, Benjamin came back to Lexington when his mother's parents died, and he inherited their estate."

"Where was that?"

Clay chuckled. "A little place you might be familiar with. It's now known as Rutherford Commons."

Mary Claire turned so that she faced him. "Why did I never know any of this?"

"Every family's got skeletons, Mary Claire. Root around too much in the family history, you tend to dig up things you'd rather not."

She settled back against the bench.

"Mary Claire, if I'd known about Anna Bell, that she was a McCullough, I would have been mad as hell, but I wouldn't have made you marry John." He put his arm around her shoulders as she leaned over against him. "That was wrong in a whole lot of ways."

Mary Claire snuggled into his shoulder. His jacket smelled like 'Old Spice', hay, and tobacco. "It wasn't so bad, Daddy. John was a good man. And I did get Sissy out of the deal."

"God help us," he groaned.

Mary Claire shivered. Clay had more to say, she was sure. She could sense his struggle to verbalize all that he was feeling. She stuck her hands further into her pockets and waited for her father to continue. It didn't take long.

"You know, I always knew what to do where the boys were concerned. Even when they were rebelling I was always able to come to some kind of understanding with them. But I never knew what to do with you. I thought if I let you work in the barns with us, keep you close physically, I'd be able to figure you out someday."

"Of course, your mother was always mad at me over that. She thought you ought to be sitting in the parlor writing letters or pouring tea. When you run off to Louisville, Caroline about drove me crazy wanting me to make you come home. She was furious when I fixed up the top floor of that building and let you live there. When you finally did come home, I guess insisting that you marry John was her way of making sure you'd stay put."

He was quiet. They sat in darkness, surrounded by the sounds of night—the whistle of a distant train, the baying of a coon hound, the hoot of a barn owl—until Clay finally spoke again.

"What I'm trying to say, but taking the long way around to get there, is that if you want to marry Graham McCullough, go ahead. You have my blessing."

Mary Claire couldn't talk. She wanted to, needed to. But she had so much emotion roiling inside her that she knew she'd end up sounding like a blubbering idiot if she tried. So she sat there leaning against her father, both of them staring at the night.

"Look!" Clay raised his arm toward the heavens. "A shooting star."

It was appropriate, Mary Claire thought. Even the heavens fell at the sound of a Rutherford welcoming a McCullough into the fold.

Chapter Twenty-Two

Ben, Hank and Mary Claire hosted a surprise eightieth birthday celebration for their father at the country club. Clay tried to act perturbed.

"Damn fool nonsense. All this fuss," he whispered when Mary Claire clasped her arms around his neck to kiss his cheek.

"Happy birthday, Daddy." She could see the beginning of a smile when she pulled away from him.

Caroline held court from an arm chair in the center of the room for her first public outing since her heart surgery.

Mary Claire steered Clay toward a chair close to Caroline's where they had placed the gifts for him to open.

"Mary Claire, I don't need more stuff," he growled when he saw the pile of packages.

"Then we'll give it all to Goodwill tomorrow. Just be polite and open the packages for now."

She turned the supervision of the gift opening over to Ben and went to stand by her new sister-in-law. Ben and Judy had gone to Nashville for Valentine's weekend and came home married. Caroline was still peeved that they hadn't had a proper church wedding.

Clay opened all the packages without offending any of the givers for which Mary Claire was immensely thankful—no small feat for him. Ben shoved a stack of cards closer to Clay.

"Hell, Ben, I can't read these. I didn't bring my glasses."

Ben stood up and looked at his sister. "Mary Claire, come here."

She took Ben's place at Clay's side. "Okay, Daddy, you open the cards and hand them to me and I'll read them."

They were nearing the bottom of the stack. Clay flexed his hands and picked up the next one. He pulled the card from the envelope and didn't notice when something fell to the floor. Hank reached over and picked up the object that had fallen and handed it to Clay.

It was the size of a picture, but all swirly, in black and white. Clay turned it every way possible and finally handed it to Mary Claire along with the card. "What in the hell is that supposed to be?"

She glanced at the card and immediately recognized the handwriting. She smiled and then looked at the small black and white image. Tears welled up in her eyes. She had to ask for a tissue to dry her eyes before she could read this one. It was from Anna Bell.

Grandpop,

Sorry we couldn't be there for the party, but we're getting everything finalized and arranged for the move back. I asked Mother what I should send for a gift and she said you'd probably just prefer a card. So here is your card and your gift. I know you're wondering, so I'll explain. This is an ultrasound picture of the baby. Your great-grandson who will be named Henry Clay Rutherford Kemme. Happy Birthday!

With love,
Anna Bell & Brian

Ben and Judy volunteered to take Caroline home so Clay could stay a bit longer. His socializing had also been curtailed by Caroline's infirmity.

Mary Claire walked Sissy and Laura Ellen to the door and said goodbye to them, then turned toward the cluster of people in the lounge area of the banquet room. Few of the guests had left, most everyone was gathered around Clay, talking horses.

Mary Claire slipped her arm inside Graham's and leaned against him. He glanced at her and smiled, then removed his arm from her grasp and draped it across her shoulders just as Carson Hunt spoke to him.

"McCullough, any truth to the rumor, you're hiding out a ringer in Scotland?"

All eyes turned to Graham. "What do you mean, Mr. Hunt?"

Carson Hunt was in his late sixties. His stable had produced a number of graded stakes winners, one Preakness winner and one Derby second place finisher in its brief but storied history.

"You know damn well what I mean. I was in the UK last week. I heard you've got a filly you're keeping under wraps over there. A three-year old that just happens to be the great-granddaughter of Bluegrass Bountiful?"

"No goddamn way!" Clay exploded. "I don't know about any of Bountiful's progeny being in the UK."

Carson, still looking at Graham, continued. "Could make a great story line for the Derby. If you put her in to run against Clay's horse, Sir Walker. The television people just eat that stuff up. Bountiful's great-granddaughter and great-great-grandson going head-to-head trying to win the race their old granddaddy did back in the seventies. Yes sir, make a great story. By the way, what's her name?"

Graham pulled Mary Claire tighter against him and waited for a moment before he spoke. "I was at Churchill Downs the year Bluegrass Bountiful won the Derby. It was one of the most memorable days of my life."

Mary Claire dipped her head. She noticed he only said he'd been at the race, not that he'd seen it. He hadn't seen anything but the backs of other people's heads and her legs draped across his shoulders. Her face felt like a red-hot glowing coal. She hoped everyone was watching Graham and not looking at her.

Graham continued to speak. "The filly's name is Mary, Queen of Scots. Her dam was a brood that had been sold off with a mixed lot after a particularly nasty divorce proceeding by an ex-wife who didn't know a thoroughbred from a pack mule. The mare was old, she'd fallen under the radar. So when we found out about her, we bought her. I believe she was originally sold at Keeneland in '90. Out of Miss Milly by Lexington Bounty."

Mary Claire looked up and saw her father nodding his head. Evidently Graham's recitation of his horse's parentage had convinced Clay. Everyone started firing questions at Graham. Everyone but Hank. He was looking at her—with a great big grin on his face.

****

Graham leaned against the white rail fence watching Sir Walker's morning exercise run. Though Sir Walker's pedigree showed Bluegrass Bountiful one generation farther removed than did Mary, Queen of Scots', both lines still showed the long sleek withers and powerful hind quarters that Bountiful had possessed.

Hank hooked his right foot on the bottom rail of the fence and leaned in beside Graham.

"Checking out the competition?"

Graham nodded. "It's awfully convenient having it right outside my back door. No effort at all to spy properly."

"You decided yet if you're going to run the filly?"

"No. Hamish wants to wait another week or so before he decides. He's still a bit concerned about having her obligated to run in the Preakness and the Belmont after she wins the Derby." He stole a glance at Hank's face and saw the smile he expected.

"Going to cost you a pile of money to put her in that late." Hank stuck his hand into his pocket. "But then I guess that don't matter much to someone who don't even mention that he's lost this." Hank held his hand out in front of Graham.

Graham glanced down. Hank was holding Mary Claire's engagement ring.

"When did you find it?"

"The other day. I came out the door off the back terrace and walked past the pool through the field headed for the lower barns. It about blinded me when the sun caught it."

Graham didn't say anything, just nodded his head.

"I though about giving it to Mary Claire. Then I remembered she gave it back, so it rightfully belongs to you again."

Graham took the ring from Hank's outstretched hand. He stared at it for a minute and then closed his hand around the metal and stone, remembering the last time he'd held it. "I just hauled off and threw it that night, as far as I could."

They watched Sir Walker pass by them again.

"Was that when you met her? At the Derby the year Bountiful won?"

"Yes. Spent the weekend with her. I didn't even know her name, but after just three days, I already knew I wanted to marry her."

"Why in the hell didn't you know her name?"

Graham laughed. "She wouldn't tell me. She already knew who I was. She figured if I found out she was a Rutherford, it would change things. She was working on a sculpture of Annabel Lee so I called her Annabel the whole weekend."

"I always wondered where in the world that name came from. Everyone else was naming little girls April or Stacy back then, and Mary Claire comes up with an oddball moniker like Anna Bell? Didn't make sense. No one in our family or John's was ever named Anna Bell." Hank turned his head, squinting into the morning sun as he looked at Graham. "Why didn't you marry her then?"

Graham looked out across the exercise track to the rolling lush green fields beyond and remembered the smothering green of the Amazon jungle. He told Hank the story of his father's disappearance and his fruitless six-month search followed by another when he returned to Louisville. "I couldn't believe it when I walked through that barn at Keeneland and saw her standing there with dirt smeared on her face and pieces of straw sticking in her hair, shoveling horse droppings. It was the most beautiful sight I'd ever seen."

They watched the horse as it ran past them again. When Sir Walker was on the back side of the track, Graham looked at the ring in his hand and then turned to look at Hank. "You think it'd do any good for me to ask her again to marry me?"

Hank's expression was serious. "I don't know. Mary Claire's always played it close to the vest. Can't ever tell what she's thinking. Ben and me raised all kinds of hell while we were growing up. Mary Claire's a hell-raiser at heart too, but Mom was always so goddamned insistent that everything she did had to be proper. John was the same way."

"With a Mother like Sissy? That's surprising."

"John was a real Beaumont. Sissy's a universe in and of herself. A force of nature that shapes everything around her and sweeps all that lays in her path along with her."

Graham smiled.

Hank looked at Graham and then continued. "That little hell-raiser spent twenty-five years toeing the line. After the birth of her very premature baby that for some reason seemed to be full-sized, not one hint of impropriety marked her existence." Hank held his arms up over his head and stretched. "I think for now, she's just enjoying this scandalous living in sin."

"I'm going to ask her anyway."

The exercise rider was taking Sir Walker off the track, headed for the barn.

"Go ahead." Hank said, himself headed for the barn. "Just don't be surprised if she says no."

****

They celebrated Easter at Beaumont House. Sissy insisted.

"At this point every celebration could be my last. Besides, me hosting dinner will give Caroline more of a break. She won't have to be worried with all the fuss of getting ready."

Sissy didn't worry with the fuss either. She left it to Ida, who more and more called the florist and the caterer and then supervised when the workers showed up.

"How is it we socialize with the Beaumonts more now than when you and John were married?" Ben sat down on the sofa by Mary Claire and sunk his fork into a piece of mile-high lemon chiffon pie.

She raised her eyebrows at him and her voice was barely above a whisper. "Don't complain. At least we're out from under Mother's thumb for one more holiday."

"Yeah, that's not going to last much longer." Hank stuck a finger into the side of Ben's pie and came away with a good size taste which he promptly stuck into his mouth. "She's chomping at the bit to regain control."

Judy came in and sat down by Ben. "You three look like you're conspiring."

"Not really." Mary Claire said. "Just trying not to get caught blaspheming."

Vicky came into the room carrying a basket filled with hand-dipped chocolates. Laura Ellen was close on her heels.

"Mary Claire, you might want to go rescue Mr. McCullough. Your daddy has him cornered in the kitchen, haranguing him over his breeding stock."

Hank stood up and waved Mary Claire back down. "I'll go." He glanced at his watch. "I need to find my wife anyway so we can say our goodbyes. We promised to stop by her brother's house this afternoon."

"I believe you'll find her in the front room." Laura Ellen offered.

"Thank you." Hank nodded. "See you all later."

Hank could hear Clay long before he got to the kitchen.

"I still say no English stock's got the stamina to run with our Kentucky 'breds. They didn't keep the strength of the Arabian's in the English lines. Let 'em get soft. Few of the Irish lines may do all right, but I'll tell you, the studs coming out of South Africa. You mark my words, they're the ones we need to be watching."

"Hey, Dad." Hank interrupted. Clay stopped talking and turned toward Hank. "Graham, I believe Mary Claire is looking for you."

Graham raised his eyebrows and smiled. "I'd better go see what she wants." He got away before Clay could start in on him again.

Chapter Twenty-Three

Graham flew to London on the Wednesday after Easter and stayed for two weeks. Mary Claire spent the time packing up and cleaning out her house in town. Sissy had decided to buy the house to give to Macy, Laura Ellen's daughter, as a wedding gift.

Mary Claire supposed she and Graham would move back to the penthouse apartment after Anna Bell and Brian got settled in at Castleton Downs.

She was in the basement, on a step-stool, clearing the top shelf in a storage area on the far side of the furnace. She pulled a cardboard box from the shelf. It slipped from her grasp and fell, scattering its contents across the floor. She sighed and got off the stool to clean up the mess.

The first thing she picked up was a length of red silk, a scarf from the Rutherford Commons racing silks. Under the scarf was an envelope containing the black and white photographs of Graham she'd taken that night in the diner thirty years ago, after the Derby. Burl had given them to her when he'd had the film developed. She felt a pang of guilt that she'd kept them all these years here in John's house. She shuffled through them once and then again. She put them back in the envelope and stuck it, along with the scarf, in the pocket of her sweater.

****

Graham got back two days ahead of schedule. He'd spent the last twelve days cooped-up in the little apartment above Castleton-McCullough's London office. It was a place he used to stay if there was a corporate or weather emergency or if he'd worked so late that it didn't make sense to even go home. It was meant for an overnight stay, not a two-week encampment.

The inconvenience had been worth it. He, Hamish, Jamie, the accountants and the board had worked a couple of marathon sessions but had managed to finalize the transfer of corporate control to Jamie and to split Hamish's duties into three separate jobs. Graham and Hamish were now reduced to being merely members of the board of directors, albeit permanent ones.

Graham found Mary Claire at the apartment in her bathrobe, getting dressed for an early evening fund-raiser.

"Do you have to do anything at the fund-raiser?"

"Yes."

"What?"

"Give them money."

"Okay, smart ass." He smacked her on the behind. "But you don't have to be there in person to do that, do you?"

"Well, no, but I have already paid for dinner and it's always really good. You could come with me."

"No thank you. I've been cooped up for two weeks. I want to get outside in this fantastic weather. London was damp and cold. Let's drive out to Castleton Downs."

"Okay. Let me get dressed and then call Judy to tell her I won't be at the fund-raiser."

"Late April had turned out to be particularly warm. The redbud trees that bordered the road on the drive out to the farm were in full bloom, and the dogwoods just starting to bleach white.

Mary Claire turned to study Graham's profile. It was unusual for them to be riding together. They usually met somewhere after driving separately.

"Do you remember the first time we drove out here together?" Her voice was teasing.

"Oh yes." He glanced at her. "I really thought I'd blown it that night. I didn't think I'd ever see you again after the way you stomped off."

"Did you really and truly think you were going to end up on that bed with me?"

"Hell, yes!" His eyes sparkled. "Those three days in Louisville were my only frame of reference where you were concerned. I was game. I figured you would be too. I mean it wasn't like you didn't enjoy yourself that weekend." He reached across the seat and squeezed her hand.

They rode the rest of the way in comfortable silence, each lost in their own memories.

For the middle of the afternoon, Castleton Downs seemed deserted. Sir Walker had been moved back to Rutherford Commons in preparation for the Derby and Mary, Queen of Scots wasn't due to arrive until the following week.

Graham and Mary Claire walked all the way down the service road, past the last barn, until it turned from a two-lane paved surface into a gravel covered single lane. They kept walking even after the gravel road disintegrated into a path created by the wear of tire tracks. They walked through the stand of trees into a clearing that bordered the banks of a small creek that meandered across the landscape.

"Are we still on Castleton Downs' property?" Mary Claire stopped. They'd been walking for twenty minutes.

"We are. We're only about a third of the way to the property line going in this direction." Graham raised his arm and pointed to a stand of trees far to her right. "That tree line is the northern border. The fields across there is where they're going to start planting for the vineyard."

He turned back toward Mary Claire. She had her eyes closed, her head leaned back, and a big smile on her face.

"What are you doing?"

"Smelling." She inhaled deeply. "I love the scent of spring. It's so full of promise, infinite possibilities."

He stepped in front of her and lowered his head until his lips touched hers. The kiss was sweet, familiar.

"See what I mean?" She said when the kiss ended. "One minute I'm standing here in the middle of nowhere with my eyes closed. Next thing I know Prince Charming is kissing me."

"Prince Charming?"

"Yes."

"I've always seen myself more as the Knight in Shining Armor."

"Whatever." She raised her arms up to circle his neck and pressed on the back of his head trying to lower his mouth to hers again. This time the kiss was more demanding.

Graham pulled at the tail of her unbuttoned sweater from both sides to move it from between them, then slid his hands up under her shirt. The warm scent of her perfumed body drifted to his nostrils.

"You smell better than springtime." His voice was raspy, filled with his need of her. Graham unsnapped her jeans. He held on to one side and pulled the zipper tab all the way down then slid his hand inside. He started laughing. "I thought you only went commando when you were in a hurry."

"I discovered I liked it. It's so liberating."

He pulled away from her and took his jacket off. He spread it on the ground and then dipped his hand into her jeans again. "I like it too."

His jacket proved to be large enough to accommodate Mary Claire's bare butt and his knees on either side of her. Their coupling was quick but still satisfying. Graham rolled over onto the ground on his back.

Mary Claire sat up, laughing as she pulled leaves and bits of grass from her hair.

"What's so funny?"

"Us. We look like a couple of teenagers who couldn't wait." She still had her shirt on. Her bra was fastened but was resting in a bunched up band above her breasts. Her jeans were around her ankles and her socks and boots still intact.

Graham was nearly the same. His slacks were dangling at the top of his right boot, the left leg turned inside out. He'd only kicked off one boot and paused long enough to take one leg out of his pants so he could straddle her more easily.

"It must be those infinite possibilities of spring. I *feel* like a teenager." He said.

She scooted over beside him, making sure she kept her behind on his jacket. "Me too. I've never done it outside before."

He laughed at her obvious appreciation of the experience. "Kind of fun, don't you think?"

"Uh-huh."

Graham felt his pulse quicken as he thought about the ring in his pocket. He hoped it hadn't fallen out. It wasn't the same one, not the ostentatious diamond he'd given her before. That wasn't who Mary Claire was. That one had been more about him, staking his claim, marking his territory. This one, he'd bought in a little shop in London four days ago. It was a wedding ring, rimmed with diamonds and rubies. Subtle and sparkling at the same time, just like Mary Claire.

He reached over and pulled her closer. "Mary Claire, there's something I've been thinking about for a while."

"What?"

"I think we should build a little house back here. That's why I wanted to walk out here, so you could see it. I know you don't really like living in the apartment and now that you're selling your house in town…"

She craned her neck, to look at her surroundings, then twisted so that she was looking at him. "Right here."

"Well, somewhere back here." He thought she was asking a question.

"No. I mean right here. This is the perfect place." She reached out and grabbed a broken tree branch that lay on the ground and then fished in the pocket of her sweater pulling out a red silk scarf and a white envelope. She handed the envelope to Graham. "You might enjoy these."

She tied the scarf around the tree branch, then pulled her jeans up to the bend of her knees and moved her bra back to its proper position. She raised to a kneeling position.

"I can't believe you still have these." He laughed. "God, I looked awful. I can't believe you took me home with you."

"I can't either." She nudged him over a tad and moved his jacket aside. "But then I did take in a lot of strays in those days. You were just one more bedraggled alley cat to feed." She plunged the branch into the soft earth.

Graham put the pictures back into the envelope and turned to see what she'd done.

"Right here is where we'll break ground. This very spot." She leaned over and touched the base of the branch where it met the dirt that surrounded it. "Right here, where our bodies were one with the earth."

He raised up on his knees behind her. He wrapped his arms around her and settled back on his haunches pulling her back to rest against him.

He leaned his head forward so that his mouth was close to her ear. "I have one more thing to ask."

"What?" She was tracing circles with her fingertips on his hand that splayed across her stomach.

"Mary Claire Rutherford, will you marry me?"

Her fingers stopped in mid motion.

He felt a moment of panic at her complete stillness, the memory of Hank's words echoing in his head. But when she turned to face him, all doubt drained away.

"Yes. Oh yes, Mr. McCullough. I surely will."

Chapter Twenty-Four

The First Saturday in May

Mary Claire checked her reflection in the full length mirror. She wore a sleeveless white dress, fitted at the waist with a full skirt and a matching waist length jacket with three-quarter length sleeves. It wasn't even daylight yet, but everyone was up and ready to go. They were only waiting for her.

She opened the top drawer of the dresser and picked up the white velvet drawstring pouch. She opened it to check one last time, pulled it closed, tied the string in a bow and slipped it into the pocket of her dress. That was another reason she loved this dress. It had pockets. The first reason she loved it was because it was going to be her wedding dress—at least she hoped it was.

After Graham had proposed to her, they had gone over the calendar three times trying to find a weekend that hadn't already been claimed by some other family or business event. If they wanted anyone other than themselves to attend the wedding, it would have to be the second week of next January.

Mary Claire remarked on the lack of available open calendar dates last week while she lunched with Sissy. Sissy had suggested it, a wedding at the Governor's Breakfast. Most of their family would be there today anyway, so why not take advantage of it.

Mary Claire had called Sean to ask about the annulment thing. He's assured her that it was already done. That Barbara had filed for annulment before she had remarried so Graham was also free to remarry though it would have been preferable in Sean's eyes that it be a union before God rather than a union before the governor. Maybe she should seat Sean next to her mother. They'd probably have a lot to talk about.

Sissy had gone to Frankfort yesterday to take care of things with the governor. Sissy hadn't called to report any problems so Mary Claire assumed it was a go. She smiled to herself. She was sure that Sissy's political clout alone was enough to ensure that the proper arrangements would be made, but it couldn't hurt that Ben and the governor had been roommates all thorough college.

Mary Claire turned when she heard the door open. Graham walked into the room and frowned. "I thought you were going to wear the red polka-dot thing."

"Well, I was going to, but the red in the dots is the exact same color as the Rutherford silks. I didn't want anyone to think I was being disloyal to you by trying to coordinate my outfit to the Rutherford colors, if I should have to be in the winner's circle with Sir Walker." She looked at him with an innocent smile. "I am part owner of him too. This dress will blend with the Rutherford or the McCullough silks, so I'll look good in the winner's circle either way."

"There are thirteen other horses running today. You may not have to worry about the winner's circle at all."

She slipped her feet into her white heels, picked up her gloves and hat from the bed, and stopped beside him on her way to the door. She lifted herself up on her tip toes and kissed his cheek.

"Perish the thought, my dear." She kept walking toward the door. "I'm ready."

****

They'd all spent last night at Castleton Downs, Graham, Mary Claire, Anna Bell, Brian, Hamish, Polly and her husband, Charles, and Sean and were now all loading into a limo headed for Frankfort and a private tent at the Governor's Derby Breakfast.

The pre-race festivities had turned into a media circus. Just like Carson Hunt had predicted, the television people were eating it up. Mary Claire was sure they'd interviewed everyone who had ever heard of Bluegrass Bountiful.

That is every one but Sissy. She had steadfastly refused. She'd even had Ida call the law on one television crew that hadn't vacated the premises quickly enough after she'd asked them to leave. "All those damned cameras stuck in your face. And the lights and cords everywhere. Just ruin what used to be a wonderful day," she'd complained.

Anna Bell, sitting next to Polly, was relating a conversation she'd had with Sissy two days ago.

"Grandmother said it used to always be about the horses and the food and getting dressed fit to kill. But now it's all about what celebrity shows up for the parties."

"Sissy is coming today, isn't she? Graham was still amazed at how much Anna Bell resembled Polly.

"Oh yes." Anna Bell assured him. "Actually, she's already in Frankfort. Aunt Laura drove her down last evening. She spent the night at the governor's mansion."

"Really?" Graham leaned back in the seat.

Mary Claire twisted around to look at him. "Rest assured, if this shindig was taking place in Washington, Sissy would have spent the night at the White House."

Graham chuckled. "I really don't doubt that at all."

****

The media circus was already going full tilt at the private tent that had been set up for the Rutherfords and the McCulloughs at the Governor's Derby Breakfast.

Clay and Hank were doing separate interviews on the outside of the tent, when the McCullough party came up the walk.

They walked past the entourage of reporters clustered at the entrance to the tent. Mary Claire slipped her arm from Graham's grasp and ducked inside when Graham stopped to speak to them.

Judy grabbed her and gave her a big hug as soon as she was inside. Judy was so excited she was about to explode. "You look gorgeous," she whispered, as she dragged Mary Claire to where Sissy was sitting, having a quiet conversation with a middle-aged lady.

"Mary Claire, do you know Madeline Harper, the lieutenant governor's wife?"

Mary Claire nodded. "Why yes. We met at the Heritage Commission's benefit auction last year. The one that was held in Midway."

"That's right. You bought the collection of Jesse Stuart first editions."

"And they look lovely in my library." Mary Claire's sugar sweet smile even looked sincere.

Madeline Harper stood. "Well, I should find my husband. We have to get to the Downs a little early since the governor is going to be delayed." She touched Sissy on the shoulder. "Mrs. Beaumont it was nice to see you again." She walked away.

"Ouch!" Judy laughed. "Jab, jab."

Mary Claire sat down in the chair Mrs. Harper had just vacated. "We didn't just meet at that auction. She's hated me since high school. She had a major crush on John." Mary Claire looked at Sissy's smiling face. "And she really wanted those Stuart books. I paid a fortune for them just so she couldn't have them."

"That's my girl." Sissy patted Mary Claire's hand.

Mary Claire looked at Judy then back to Sissy. "So?"

Sissy nodded. "Everything's set. As soon as we get rid of the TV vultures. I just had to pay the Franklin County license fee. The paperwork can be completed Monday.

An hour and a half later Mary Claire was starting to worry. The governor hadn't come in yet, there were still television people and reporters everywhere, and poor Hank was sitting in a chair off by himself facing the corner of the tent.

Mary Claire stopped beside Michelle and pointed to Hank. "Is he okay?"

Michelle rolled her eyes. "Well no. You know better than that." She put her arm around Mary Claire's waist. "But only because it's race day. Not because of the wedding thing."

Hank, Michelle, Judy, Sean, and Sissy were the only ones who knew. Mary Claire hadn't even told Anna Bell. Judy had been about to explode, but Mary Claire had threatened her life if she told Ben. Ben had never been able to keep anything to himself. He would have blabbed to everyone.

Just then the governor's press secretary came in with a couple of security people and three uniformed State Police officers. He walked to the front of the tent.

"May I have everyone's attention, please. We'd like for all the reporters, television, and newspaper people to leave now. The Rutherfords and the McCulloughs have requested some private time together before they leave for Louisville."

Mary Claire had been watching the press secretary and hadn't even noticed that the governor had entered the tent. He was by the doorway talking to Ben. She scanned the crowd, looking for Graham. She spotted him across the way, talking to Hamish and Sean.

When all the media people had gone, the governor walked to the front of the tent. He clapped his hands together to get everyone attention.

"Folks, we're doing something a little special here this morning." He looked around until he found Mary Claire. "Mary Claire. Mr. McCullough. Would you all come up here for a minute?"

Mary Claire waited until Graham's eyes met hers before she started walking. They met in front of the governor.

The governor spoke quietly to the two of them for a moment. Graham let out a hardy laugh and started nodding.

"By all means, sir. It would be an honor." He reached out to shake the governor's hand. "But I don't have the…"

Mary Claire slipped her hand into the pocket of her dress and pulled out the small velvet pouch. "I brought them." She opened the bag and let the two rings spill into her palm.

"Ladies and gentlemen, would you all gather around?" the governor's voice carried through the tent. "We're about to have a wedding."

It only took ten minutes, start to finish, and that was with a two-minute interruption for laughter when Graham couldn't remember all his names. He could only come up with two of the three that had been added at his baptism. Polly came to his rescue.

Hank gave Mary Claire a crushing hug. "Congratulations, kid. Be happy." He then turned to Graham and stuck out his hand. Graham clasped it. "I'm glad I was wrong." He broke into a big smile and slapped Graham on the back.

Hamish hurriedly offered his congratulations before he and Hank ran out of the tent together to catch a chopper ride to Louisville.

The governor watched their hasty exit. He offered his own best wishes and then said goodbye to Sissy and Clay and Caroline. He shook Ben's hand. "Your family still takes the cake. Never a dull moment when the Rutherford's are around. I'd better get out of here myself. I need to catch a ride to Louisville too."

"Yeah." Ben nodded. "Crazy." And then called out to the governor's back. "See you this afternoon. In the winner's circle."

Anna Bell hugged her mother and then her father. "Why didn't you tell us you were going to do this?"

"I wasn't sure we were going to be able to, until we got here. But I did ask Sissy to make the arrangements with the governor."

"Then why in the world did you have any doubt?" Graham laughed as he leaned over and kissed Anna Bell on the cheek.

"Just being cautious."

Clay and Caroline stopped to speak to the newly weds.

Caroline touched her cheek to Mary Claire's. "Congratulations, Mary Claire. I hope this makes you happy."

Mary Claire felt her hackles raise, until she looked into her mother's eyes.

"Really happy." Caroline finished.

She meant it and Mary Claire knew she meant it. "It does, Mother. Thank you."

Caroline patted her hand then reached over to take Graham's hand. "Welcome to the family, Mr. McCullough."

"Thank you."

Clay put his arms around Mary Claire. She laid her head on his shoulder. "Be happy, baby." He patted her on the back.

"I am, Daddy."

"God, you've been keeping company with Sissy too long, pulling a stunt like this." He pulled away from her and held his hand out to Graham. "McCullough, you don't treat her right, you'll answer to me."

Graham took his hand and shook it. "I know that, sir."

Clay smiled at him and then turned on his heel toward the tent entrance. His voice boomed through the nearly empty tent. "Won't be much of a wedding present. Getting your ass whipped at the track." He was laughing as he went toward the waiting car.

Sissy was the last to offer congratulations. "Well, I'm glad we finally got this accomplished." She pointed toward the doorway where Ida was entering the tent. "Ida's come to take me back home."

"You're not coming to the race?" Disappointment was evident in Graham's voice.

"No. I'm already worn out. I think I'll enjoy it a lot more in my front room watching on the television. Besides," she laughed, "there I can drink all the bourbon I want without someone sticking them damn weeds in it."

Graham chuckled. "Be careful, I've done that before."

She nodded. "So have I my boy, so have I."

Mary Claire wrapped her arms around Sissy. "Thank you, Sissy. For everything."

"You're welcome, darling."

Mary Claire stepped back so Graham could say goodbye to Sissy. He leaned down and kissed her cheek.

Sissy reached out for Graham's hand. She stared into his face for a full thirty seconds before she spoke. "John would have liked you." She nodded her head. "And he loved her daughter."

"Thank you." Graham mouthed the words.

Ida offered Sissy her arm and headed her toward the door.

Alone in the tent, Graham wrapped Mary Claire in his arms while she had a complete melt down.

****

Mary Claire redid her makeup in the limo on the short ride to the airfield. They were all going to Louisville by helicopter. Getting to the racetrack was so much nicer now that they'd built the helipad on top of the new building at Churchill Downs.

Even though they'd always been able to use the private entrance into the race track, just getting there on Derby day through all the traffic was hell.

Mary Claire, Graham, and Anna Bell were the last of their group waiting at the airfield.

"McCullough." Mary Claire's eyes sparkled as she spoke. "You're about to have a real Derby experience today."

"You mean I didn't have one before?"

She laughed and shook her head. "I hope you won't be disappointed, though. There aren't any slip-n-slides in the skyboxes."

"Won't matter." He crossed his arms over his chest. "I won't be stripping down to my skivvies, trying to impress hot babes in short-shorts anyway."

Anna Bell frowned at them. "What in the world are you two talking about?"

The chopper that would carry them to Louisville set down on the lading pad. The field attendant waved for them to come out of the waiting area. Anna Bell walked ahead of her parents. Graham took Mary Claire's hand and squeezed it.

"It's a long story, baby. We'll tell you about it someday." Mary Claire swung their clasped hands to and fro between them.

"Yeah." Graham said. "Someday when you're older." He stopped the motion of their hands and brought them up to his lips, placing a kiss on the back of Mary Claire's. Then he let go.

Anna Bell smiled before she rolled her eyes at him and then let him help her into the chopper. Graham and Mary Claire were still laughing as they climbed in behind her.

The chopper took off and headed toward Churchill Downs, toward the place that had given birth to this fledgling family.

The End

About the Author

Lozi Hart grew up along the Ohio River in the Appalachian foothills of eastern Kentucky. She has studied music, art, architecture, interior design and anthropology. She adores old houses and loves writing about the people who inhabit them, whether their residence is in body or in spirit. Her first novel, Bluegrass Bountiful, will be published by Turquoise Morning Press in April of 2011.

Lozi's website is www.lozihart.com

Stories by Lozi Hart

"The Unhaunted House"
in Something Spooky This Way Comes

Thank you!

For purchasing this Lozi Hart novel from
Turquoise Morning Press.

We invite you to visit our Web site to learn more about
our quality Trade Paperback and eBook selections.

www.turquoisemorningpress.com
www.sapphirenightsbooks.com

You can also find our books at many digital and print
retailers, including:

Amazon
Barnes and Noble
All Romance eBooks
OmniLit
Bookstrand
Diesel eBooks
Kobo
Sony Reader Store
Apple iBooks Store
Smashwords
Coffee Time Romance eBookstore
1PlaceForRomance
1EroticaEbooks
XinXii
Owjo

Turquoise Morning Press

Because every good beach deserves a book.

www.turquoisemorningpress.com

~~~~~

Sapphire Nights Books

Because sometimes the beach just isn't hot enough.

www.sapphirenightsbooks.com

9011812R0

Made in the USA
Charleston, SC
03 August 2011